Praise for Rose Pressey
and
If You've G...

"Rose Pressey's books a...

"A delightful protagonist, intriguing twists, and a fashionista ghost combine in a hauntingly fun tale. Definitely haute couture."   —Carolyn Hart

"If you're a fan of vintage clothing and quirky ghosts, Rose Pressey's *If You've Got It, Haunt It* will ignite your passion for fashion and pique your otherworldly interest. Wind Song, the enigmatic cat, adds another charming layer to the mystery."   —Denise Swanson

"*If You've Got It, Haunt It* is a stylish mystery full of vintage fashions and modern flair, with a dash of Rose Pressey's trademark paranormal wit for that final touch of panache. Chic and quirky heroine Cookie Chanel and a supporting cast of small-town Southern characters are sure to charm lovers of high fashion and murderous hi-jinks alike."   —Jennie Bentley

"Absolutely delightful! Prolific author Rose Pressey has penned a delightful mystery full of Southern charm, vintage fashion tips, a ghostly presence and a puzzler of a mystery. With snappy dialogue and well-drawn characters in a lovely small town setting, this thoroughly engaging story has it all."   —Jenn McKinlay

"Fun, fast-paced, and fashionable, *If You've Got It, Haunt It* is the first in Rose Pressey's appealing new mystery series featuring clever vintage-clothing expert Cookie Chanel. A charming Southern setting, an intriguing murder, a stylish ghost, a tarot-reading cat, and a truly delectable detective combine to make Ms. Pressey's new Haunted Vintage series a sheer delight."   —Kate Carlisle

"Prolific mystery author Pressey launches a cozy series with an appealing protagonist who is as sweet as a Southern accent. The designer name-dropping and shopping tips from Cookie add allure for shopaholics."   —*Library Journal*

All Dressed Up and No Place to Haunt

Rose Pressey

KENSINGTON PUBLISHING CORP.
http://www.kensingtonbooks.com

KENSINGTON BOOKS are published by

Kensington Publishing Corp.
119 West 40th Street
New York, NY 10018

All Kensington Titles, Imprints, and Distributed Lines are available at special quantity discounts for bulk purchases for sales promotions, premiums, fund-raising, and educational or institutional use. Special book excerpts or customized printings can also be created to fit specific needs. For details, write or phone the office of the Kensington special sales manager: Kensington Publishing Corp., 119 West 40th Street, New York, NY 10018, attn: Special Sales Department, Phone: 1-800-221-2647.

Kensington and the K logo Reg. U.S. Pat & TM Off.

ISBN-13: 978-1-61773-251-5
ISBN-10: 1-61773-251-6
First Kensington Mass Market Edition: July 2015

eISBN-13: 978-1-61773-252-2
eISBN-10: 1-61773-252-4
First Kensington Electronic Edition: July 2015

10 9 8 7 6 5 4 3 2 1

Printed in the United States of America

To my son, the kindest, most wonderful person
I've ever known. He motivates me every day.
He's the love of my life.

Chapter 1

Seeing a ghost didn't shock me as much the second time around. Don't get me wrong—it was still strange and a little unnerving, but overall, I thought I handled it quite nicely.

My day had started out to be a fantastic one, but it had gone downhill quickly. A sweeping saga titled *Moonlight and Magnolias* was being shot at Fairtree Plantation, and I'd been invited to watch. The 1850 antebellum mansion made a gorgeous backdrop for the film. Maple, oak, magnolia, and dogwood trees covered the twelve-acre estate. The three-story brick home sat at the end of a tree-lined drive.

Silence surrounded the set as I watched the

actors bring the script to life. The lead characters were embraced in a passionate kiss. Of course, ten seconds ago they had been arguing. As the gorgeous Nicole Silver wrapped her arms around her hunky costar, Preston Hart, I noticed the sparkle of the ring she wore. Wow, it was huge. I wondered if it was her own or a stage prop.

I'd never been this close to the action before. I'd once watched a movie being filmed while on vacation in New York City, but we'd been held back by barricades. Now I had a front-row seat for all the action. I was thrilled that I'd managed to get on the set's special guest list. Apparently, helping the film crew with their vintage costumes had perks. My hometown of Sugar Creek, Georgia, had been abuzz since the director had decided to shoot part of his new movie right here in our little town.

It's Vintage, Y'All was the name of my clothing boutique, located in the historic section of town. Since I'd started blogging about my great vintage finds, I'd gotten quite the following of readers. It hadn't taken long before a few movies had asked for my advice with their costumes. This was the biggest film so far though. Nicole Silver and Preston Hart had the kind of star quality that the media loved. I'd read in the tabloids that they were dating in real life.

I had been beyond excited when asked to help with their costumes. Nicole's shiny blond hair cascaded to her shoulders and had been styled like Veronica Lake's, with a peekaboo bang on one side. The black-and-white Christian Dior dress that I'd selected for her hugged her curves in all the right places. Her full red lips seemed to be in a constant pouting position. Preston was tall, dark, and handsome, with strong cheekbones and chiseled features. I'd give anything for his thick eyelashes—even my most recent acquisition, a 1960s Gucci handbag. He wore black trousers and a crisp white shirt with a red-and-ivory small paisley wide swing tie.

Fashion is my passion. I love what Coco Chanel said—"Elegance does not consist in putting on a new dress." And that was why I wore an Eisenhower-era outfit today. Okay, maybe that wasn't exactly what she'd meant, but nevertheless, it was what I'd gotten from the quote. My name happened to be Cookie Chanel. Funny, right? We weren't related, as far as I knew. When I'd shown such an interest in fashion, I'd been given the clever moniker of Cookie by my granny, instead of Coco, because it fit so well with Chanel—and, I admit, I really loved cookies as a child and I still do. The name fits me, so I still use it to this day.

The movie was set partly in the forties and partly in the present day. I'd had a wonderful time gathering the outfits for the actors. Of course, I had to dress the part too. After all, vintage was my thing. Today, I wore a rayon/chiffon blend red-and-white polka-dot dress. The fitted bodice came down into a princess waist. It had double straps on the shoulders and a pretty red bow in front. I matched it with a red clutch purse and straw wedge heels with a tiny red trim along the edges.

It was hard to look glamorous when your hair was plastered to your head from the relentless heat though. Living in Georgia, that was part of life. But no matter what, I made the best of it.

Nicole and Preston finished their scene, disengaging from their embrace and moving apart, their hands touching until they separated. It would be the last take for the day. I intended to stay until I absolutely had to leave. My visit to the set had been so exciting that I didn't want it to end.

Shiloh Northcutt, the costume director, approached. She wore white knee-length shorts and a plain white T-shirt. She had definitely dressed for comfort, but she made it look glamorous nonetheless, with a Louis Vuitton leopard-print scarf and strappy, red high-wedged espadrilles. Wisps of auburn hair framed her slender face.

"Cookie, you've been a lot of help and the costumes were a huge success. I hope you had a fun time today." She looked at her oversized white rhinestone watch. It looked like it could belong to the captain of a spaceship. Next to it a tattoo of a red rose decorated her pale skin.

"I had a fantastic time." I'd barely finished the sentence when Shiloh walked off to greet someone else.

Her abrupt departure was a bit rude, but I figured she was just distracted by all the action. Now that filming was over, I decided to take a walk around the property. I'd never been to the plantation before, and I'd always wanted to get a closer look.

The smell of honeysuckle drifted across the

warm summer air as I stepped through the flower garden. A moss-covered stone path led to a patio surrounded by rose bushes. Beyond the flowers, tall hedges provided a green shield from the rest of the property. Moving over to a finely carved wooden bench, I sat down and inhaled the sweet floral perfume. Voices soon caught my attention.

I leaned to my right, hoping to hear what was being said. If you want to call me a snoop, go ahead. I just couldn't resist, especially with celebrities on the loose. My grandma used to say that I was as curious as a cat in a bird feeder, and I guess she was right. The words were too muffled, so I pushed to my feet and headed toward the sound. When I reached the hedges, I realized the conversation was being held just on the other side. I eased over to the edge and peeked around.

Nicole and Preston were facing each other. Her arms were crossed in front of her waist in a defensive stance. This definitely wasn't a scene from the movie. She glared at her costar. When he reached out and touched her arm, she jerked away, and I heard the phrase "with her of all people." I didn't see the sparkly ring she'd been wearing in the film scene. Maybe it was just a prop, after all. Not wanting to be caught watching their private discussion, I summoned my willpower, set aside my curiosity, inched back, and tiptoed toward the front of the plantation.

On my way back to my car, I ran into a few actors who asked me about the vintage clothing— where I found it, how I took care of it, the research

I did to assemble the outfits for the film. After speaking with them for about twenty minutes, I spotted Shiloh again. I'd forgotten to ask her when the clothing would be returned. My plan was to auction the items off and donate the proceeds to a charity. Shiloh was so engrossed in a conversation with another member of the film crew that she didn't see me walking her way. I recognized the leggy blonde she spoke to as someone who worked with Shiloh in the costume department.

As I neared the women, I heard my name. They still didn't notice that I was headed in their direction though. I stepped behind a nearby hedge and listened. If anyone saw me hiding in the bushes, they would probably think I'd lost my mind.

"Well, I'm not happy with any of the clothing that she brought," Shiloh said.

My mouth dropped. She'd acted as if she loved the items that I'd provided. Why hadn't she mentioned this to me? If she'd told me earlier, I would have been willing to work with her and get the clothing that would have made her happy.

"I guess there's nothing you can do about it now. I'm sure everything will be fine," the other woman said.

"It'll have to be." Disgust filled Shiloh's voice.

The women moved down the path in my direction, so I headed the opposite way. I didn't feel like having a confrontation. If I asked Shiloh why she didn't express her unhappiness with me about the outfits I'd selected, I would have to admit that I had spied on her conversation.

I figured I would walk a bit until they were safely gone; then I'd go back to my car and get the heck out of there. I didn't want to chance any more hiding in bushes. The third time might be one too many.

To my right I noticed a pond. It was on the edge of the Fairtree Plantation's property. I decided to walk over and take a look at it as a way to spend a few more minutes. Once I reached the water's edge, I wasn't sure what made me look to my left, but I noticed the body floating facedown on the surface right away.

I knew by the dress that it was Nicole Silver. As I ran closer, I pulled out my cell phone. Before I had a chance to dial, a scream sounded behind me. I glanced back and saw several panicked people running at full speed toward the pond. The movie director sprinted past me and jumped in the water, dragging Nicole's lifeless body onto the grass. A chill ran up my spine, and I felt tears leaping to my eyes, even though I had barely met the actress.

The white-and-black dress had been a part of the wardrobe I'd found for Nicole. A woman in the town next to ours had donated her grandmother's things for the charity auction. As I watched the surreal scene play out in front of me, I heard a woman clear her throat. I looked to my left and saw a stranger standing beside me. Her chestnut-brown hair was twisted into an updo, and she wore a pink dress in a style similar to the one that Nicole had been wearing. It wasn't a dress that I'd given the costume director. I would remember it, if it had been one of mine.

This must have been a dress that the film crew had before they arrived in Sugar Creek. It was a lovely piece, and I was a little jealous that I hadn't found it myself. The woman wearing it must have been an extra.

"This is just terrible," she said with a shake of her head.

"So sad," I agreed. "Were you in the film with her?"

"No, but that's my dress she's wearing," she said matter-of-factly.

I looked at her more closely and realized she had a translucent glow that had nothing to do with the film makeup or lighting. This was no cast extra. Her appearance seemed grainy at first, but slowly she became more solid. She was a ghost.

Oh no, not again.

Chapter 2

*Charlotte's Handy-Dandy Tips
for Navigating the Afterlife*

*The best thing to attract
the attention of the living is to make noise.
Banging and knocking on walls
seems to be effective.*

Police and other official-looking folks surrounded the area. The rest of us watched from a distance.

It had been such a lovely day, and now it had taken this tragic turn. How had Nicole fallen in the water? Had she stepped too close to the pond's edge and slipped on the wet vegetation? Had she hit her head on a rock and lost consciousness? Or did she not know how to swim?

I looked around at the shocked faces. In a million years, I knew none of them would have expected this turn of events. What would happen to the film? Nicole was the star, but would they replace her? Or just stop the film?

My mind was spinning with questions as I realized the ghost was still talking to me.

"What a tragic end to such a beautiful life," she said.

I'd learned from past experience that I couldn't answer her without a formulated strategy. Carefully positioned cell phones or newspapers usually provided good covers, but those items weren't always available when a ghost popped up. If I talked freely with the ghosts, the people around me would think that I was talking to myself. In a town as small as Sugar Creek, word would spread quickly that I was one dress short of a full boutique. I'd recently dealt with another ghost and didn't think I'd have to deal with the supernatural again. Even if I had expected another supernatural visitor, I wouldn't have thought it would happen this soon.

Among the officials I spotted the handsome Detective Dylan Valentine of the Sugar Creek Police Department. Dylan had recently moved here from Atlanta. He had investigated the last homicide investigation in our town. Unfortunately for me, I had been a part of that one. Not because I'd wanted to be involved, but because the ghost of the murdered woman, Charlotte Meadows, had refused to leave me alone until I helped find her killer. That was one reason why I didn't want to talk with this ghost—I didn't want to get roped into another postmortem quest for justice. Of course this spirit wouldn't have anything to do with this latest event. So why was she here?

Would the detective notice that I was in the crowd? I thought about trying to escape before he spotted me, but in a split second it was too late. We made eye contact. He didn't smile, but I hadn't expected him to, considering the current situation. He spoke with the police officer beside him, and the next thing I knew he was walking in my direction.

"Uh-oh," I said under my breath.

"Is there a problem?" the ghost asked. She looked at me and then followed my gaze. "Oh . . . Do you know him?"

I cast a glance her way. When I thought Dylan wasn't watching, I said, "Yes, he's a detective with the police department."

"He's the cat's meow," she whispered.

Detective Valentine was a striking man, with his dark hair and big blue eyes, but that was neither here nor there at the moment.

"Good afternoon, Cookie. I wasn't expecting to see you here." His eyes sparkled under the bright sun.

I could have said the same thing about him. After all, I hadn't expected for there to be a death on the set of the movie.

"I was here to watch the shoot. I helped with wardrobe." I motioned toward the rack of clothing behind us.

"Did you see what happened?" he asked.

I shook my head. "No, I just walked over and there she was, in the pond . . . but a little while earlier, she was talking with someone." I looked down at my feet and then back up at him. "Actually, they were arguing."

"You should tell him that I am here," the ghost said.

Oh yeah, that was exactly what I needed to do.

"In case you didn't hear me, I said if he'd like to ask me questions, I am right here. I've been on this set all day and I saw everything that has been going on. Unfortunately I was inside the building when the murder took place." She folded her arms in front of her chest and cast a stern glare my way.

I wasn't going to get into this with her right now.

"Did you tell him that she was arguing with someone? Oh yes, you did tell him. I'm sorry. Am I talking too much?"

"Yes, just a little" was what I wanted to say. But I ignored her and kept focused on the detective.

He saw some more official-looking men arriving—probably from the medical examiner's office, I guessed. "I'd better get back to work," he said and turned to walk away. "I'll be back over in a few minutes to talk with you again if that's okay?"

"Yes. That would be fine." I told myself he was just doing his job.

"Smile at the man," the ghost said. "Show him that gorgeous grin."

How did she know I had a nice smile?

When the detective had walked away, I glanced around. It seemed as if no one was looking my way, so I asked the ghost, "Who are you? And why are you here?"

"My name is Alice Neill. I would shake your hand, but you know . . ."

Yes, I was aware that if the ghost tried to shake hands with me, her hand would simply pass through mine. "Well, it's nice to meet you, Alice," I said, "but I really should be going now."

"Aren't you going to introduce yourself?" She examined me as if checking for a name tag. "Besides, you can't leave yet, the detective still wants to talk with you."

I sighed. "My name is Cookie Chanel."

Her eyes widened. "Cookie Chanel? That sounds like Coco Chanel."

"Well, you could say I was named after her." I didn't feel like getting into the details.

"You're the one responsible for the clothing on the set?"

"Yes, that's me."

"That was my dress." Alice motioned toward where Nicole had been.

I frowned at Alice.

"You look confused," she said.

"I don't understand what you mean."

"Just like I said. That was my dress. The one that the actress was wearing. It was mine. And one of my favorites, I might add."

This day had taken a bizarre turn, and it just kept getting weirder.

"The dress is why I'm here," she said. "I loved

fashion when I was alive, so I like to stay close to my treasures. Of course I love fashion now too, but I don't get to shop often." She chuckled.

"That dress can't be yours," I said. "It was donated by a woman in Belleville."

She looked pleased. "That's my granddaughter."

"You don't look old enough to have a granddaughter. You can't be any older than me."

"How old are you?" she asked.

"I'm twenty-nine."

"You look younger. But yes, I do look twenty-five, don't I?" she asked with a smile.

The more she talked, the more befuddled I became.

"So how can that be your dress?" I scanned the area to see if anyone was watching.

Detective Valentine glanced my way again. Thank goodness he hadn't spotted me talking to myself.

"I look as I did when I was young."

Chapter 3

Cookie's Savvy Vintage Fashion Shopping Tips

Do you plan on collecting items?
You should research the designer
or time period you plan to collect
before heading out to the stores.

I'd learned a few things about how being a spirit worked when I'd run into the ghost of Charlotte Meadows. Things like the fact that walking through doors was optional. Ghosts still did it, but they didn't have to. Now I was finding out that ghosts could take on the appearance they had when they were younger. I wondered what age I'd pick if I were a ghost. Probably the age I was now. Twenty-nine was a good age. I'd finally learned how to apply my makeup well, so that counted for something. I'd always had a little too much eyeliner when I was younger.

The ghost was still standing next to me. To be

honest, I didn't know quite what to say to her. I should be used to talking with ghosts by now, although chatting to one ghost didn't make me an expert by any means.

"What do we do now?" Alice asked.

What was she asking me for? I didn't have the answer. I watched in stunned silence as the police and other experts worked the crime scene. Detective Valentine looked my away again.

How had I managed to be at the scene of a crime again? He finished the conversation with another officer and headed in my direction.

"Oh, that handsome man is watching you. Is he your husband?" Alice asked. "Good catch."

"He's not my anything," I said out of the corner of my mouth.

"Boyfriend?"

"He's a detective. His name is Dylan."

"Oh, well you'd better be on your best behavior. Maybe you can make him your beau."

I wasn't going to answer that one.

"How are you holding up?" Dylan asked.

"He's swoon-worthy," Alice said. "He reminds me of my dear, sweet Joe. That was my husband. Of course he had been my parents' first pick for me. Not that I didn't love the man, don't get me wrong, but . . . Well, just don't let your true love get away is all I'm saying."

Why was she telling me her life story right now? Having a conversation with a ghost and a living person at the same time wasn't easy. I'd have to ignore Alice right now.

Dylan ran his hand through his hair. "Did you see Nicole near the water? I heard you were the first to spot her."

I wondered if he was thinking about the fact that I'd been the first to find that dead man in the alley during Sugar Creek's Spring Fling festival. What an unfortunate coincidence.

"When I saw her, she was already in the water." I closed my eyes, wishing the sight from my mind. "She was floating at the surface. I guess it was already too late. That was when the director spotted her and jumped in the water to save her."

"I suppose she could have fallen in," Alice said.

Maybe it was nothing, but I felt I needed to tell Dylan about what I'd seen.

"Earlier I was walking the plantation grounds. I heard what sounded like an argument. When I peeked around the bushes, I saw Preston and Nicole. I think he may have been cheating on her." I sounded like a gossip, but Dylan needed to know every detail.

He snapped to attention. "That was right before you found her like this?"

I blinked back tears. "Yes, about thirty minutes earlier."

"Where was the location of their argument?"

I turned around to figure out just where I'd been. "Right over there."

I hadn't realized just how close to the water

we'd been. The detective stared out over the scene. I wondered what he was thinking.

"Let me know if you remember any more details."

"Yes, absolutely." My voice was low as I absorbed the chaos around me.

Unfortunately, I didn't think there were any missing facts. How had she fallen in the water? Had she been standing too close? Of course she had. How else would she fall in the water?

One of the officers called out to Dylan. "Thank you for the information, Cookie," he said to me. "I'll phone you later."

Dylan walked across the yard and over to the pond where the other officers stood. This wasn't how I thought the day would end. Poor Nicole. She was so pretty, so young. The other people who had gathered looked as stricken as I felt. Some I recognized as her fellow actors, and the others were probably extras. A couple of women hugged each other and wiped their eyes. I hadn't seen Preston since this had happened. Where was he? Did he know about this tragic accident? I hated that the thought had slipped into my mind, but what if this wasn't an accident after all? They had been arguing.

"What do you think happened to her?" Alice asked.

I jumped and clutched my chest. I'd forgotten that she'd been standing beside me.

"You're so jumpy. Maybe you need a nice cup of chamomile tea."

What I needed was not to talk to ghosts. I looked

around to see if anyone was watching before I answered.

"Well, she clearly fell into the water," I said.

Alice pursed her lips. "I saw their argument too. I'm not so sure this was an accident."

My eyes widened. "You saw the argument? Where were you?"

"I was right behind you. You just didn't pay attention."

It was a little disturbing to know that a ghost had been following me around.

"How long had you been behind me?" I asked.

Alice waved her hand. "Don't worry, I'd only walked up behind you moments earlier."

"Gee, that is a relief."

Since Dylan wasn't free to talk to me further, it was time for me to leave. Turning, I bumped into a tall blond woman. I hoped she hadn't heard my conversation with Alice. She would think that I'd lost my marbles.

When I looked at the woman's face, I realized she was the costar of the film, Jessica Duncan. The pretty blonde scowled at me.

"I'm sorry," I said.

As if she were onstage, her frown instantly turned to a smile.

"That's okay," she said sweetly.

Jessica wiped at her eyes, and the smile was gone. I didn't see tears, but since she wiped at her eyes, I assumed she'd been crying.

"This is such a tragedy. I can't believe it happened. How will the movie go on?" she asked.

Since Nicole had lost her life, I figured the last thing to worry about at the moment was the fate of the movie. "I don't know," I said.

"She's not that great of an actress." Alice moved away from Jessica.

Even the ghost didn't want to be around her.

"I was supposed to play the role that Nicole had, you know." Jessica wiped another tear. "But Nicole got the part. She was better suited for it anyway."

"She was a great actress," I said.

Jessica cast a glance at me out of the corner of her eye. "Yes, she was fabulous."

I detected some sarcasm in her tone.

"I think I'm wanted in my dressing room," she said and then walked away without saying good-bye.

How had she known she was wanted? Did she have telepathic abilities? I hadn't heard anyone call for her. Maybe she had a previous appointment.

I turned around and headed across the lush green lawn. The concrete pathway had been blocked by police so people were cutting across a yard that they normally wouldn't have walked on. I'd almost made it to the main driveway when I heard a shout.

"Hey, you. Stay off my property."

I looked around to see who the person was talking to. Since I was the only one there, I figured the comment had been directed toward me. When I glanced to my right, I spotted a woman scowling at me from beside a large oak tree. The gray-haired woman wore a giant floppy straw hat and denim overalls with a sunshine-yellow T-shirt underneath.

She pointed her finger. "You stepped over on my side."

I stopped and looked back. "I did?"

She placed her hands on her hips. "Yes, you did. My property includes that tree. When you were walking, you moved around it."

"Oh, I was avoiding a dip in the land. I didn't want to fall."

Her face was scrunched in anger. "I don't care about your excuses. Just stay on your side. Stupid movie crew has been invading my property."

"I was just on the way to my car."

"Can you please instruct everyone to stay on their side of the land?"

"You'd better do what she says, Cookie. I think she'll beat you up if you don't," Alice said.

"I just work with the costumes. I don't really have anything to do with the movie. Maybe if you talked with the producer. What's your name? I can tell him to contact you," I said.

I figured if I offered some help that would calm her down.

"My name is Vera Lemon. Those dirty rotten scum know who I am. They just don't care." Her face was red with anger.

Alice moved over beside Vera. "Now you listen here, missy. You'd better change your attitude. I won't have you talking to my friend that way." Alice yanked the hat off Vera's head and tossed it on the ground. How had she done that? Charlotte had never been able to move objects. I'd have to ask Alice how she did it.

Apparently, Alice had a bit of a temper. Unfortunately, Vera Lemon couldn't hear a word of what the ghost had said. Vera grabbed for the hat, but fell short and landed on her knees, breaking her fall with her palms. She frowned when she looked up at me, as if I had been the one to push her to the ground.

I rushed over to Vera. "Can I help you up? Are you okay?"

Vera got to her feet. "Don't touch me. I'm fine." She grabbed her hat and stuffed it back onto her head.

Alice didn't show any sign of remorse. "I just tossed her hat off, I didn't push her to the ground."

That was true.

Vera brushed grass from her pants. "Just tell everyone to say off my land."

I couldn't stop looking at how the hat was now lopsided on her head. "I'll see what I can do." I knew I couldn't do anything, but I wanted to appease Vera.

Vera glared one last time and then stomped away.

"What a very unpleasant woman," Alice said.

"Well, you didn't help by throwing her hat on the ground."

Alice straightened. "She made me mad. I didn't like the way she talked to you."

I walked toward my car as Alice kept pace with

me. "You just have to ignore people like that. Don't let them get to you."

"That's easier said than done," Alice said.

I glanced back as I headed down the driveway. Vera was nowhere in sight, and I was thankful. This would probably be the last time I was at Fairtree Plantation, so I wouldn't have to deal with her again.

Chapter 4

*Charlotte's Handy-Dandy Tips
for Navigating the Afterlife*

*Save your energy!
It's hard to capture more
and you only want to use what you've got
for the essential hauntings.*

I'd parked my Buick in the large parking lot in front of the plantation. I recognized the other vehicles involved with the film crew. There had been reports in our local paper, the *Sugar Creek Gazette*, of adding additional parking by buying adjacent land. I wondered if the purchase of that land involved Vera Lemon. For the sake of the people trying to acquire it, I hoped not.

My car stood out from all the others. It was a red 1948 Buick convertible. My grandfather left it to me, and it was probably my favorite thing in the whole world. I loved it even more than I loved chocolate, and that was saying a lot.

I opened my car door and slipped behind the wheel. I smiled every time I looked at the fuzzy dice dangling from the rearview mirror.

"Wow, this is a nice set of wheels," Alice remarked from the passenger seat.

"Thanks," I said as I cranked the engine.

After my dealings with Charlotte Meadows, it no longer surprised me that ghosts could bypass the use of doors. Alice was sitting on the front seat of my car like a teenager who was about to meet her crush for a date.

She ran her hand across the soft white leather. "I knew someone who had a car just like this one. Oh, the memories we had in that car." She giggled.

I lifted an eyebrow. "Maybe you can just keep those details to yourself."

Traffic was light as we headed back to the historic section of Sugar Creek. I couldn't wait to get back to town to share the events of the day with my best friend, Heather Sweet. She owned an occult shop right next door to my vintage-clothing boutique. She'd been the one who introduced my cat Wind Song to the Ouija board and tarot cards. But more on that later.

The historic section had brick buildings that housed a variety of stores, antique shops, and cozy cafés. Brick and stone buildings dating from the 1700s lined the streets. Sugar Creek's economy thrived, thanks to the tourists who came to enjoy the quaint downtown and the whiskey distilleries on the edge of town.

A courthouse sat in the middle of the town

square. My shop was nearby, on the edge of Main Street. I liked it because I was in close walking distance to so many things. I had to admit I looked at the old moss-covered cemetery down the street a little differently now that I was on a first-name basis with not one but two ghosts. Every time I walked past, I looked for a spirit to pop out. So far none had, thank goodness.

I pulled the Buick up in front of my store and cut the engine. Alice had been quiet on the ride there. I think she'd been daydreaming about her time spent with a special someone in a Buick just like mine.

"Nice shop," Alice said as she peered up at the sign above the door. "Is it yours?"

I nodded with a smile of pride. "Yes, she's all mine."

My store was painted a soft shade of lavender on the outside. It was made of siding, with a little porch on the front. The building looked different from the surrounding brick affairs, but it was just as old.

A pretty sign that read IT'S VINTAGE, Y'ALL hung above the door. My mother had dreamed up the name. She wasn't into fashion, but she tried to contribute all she could. Usually she tried to help by giving me the latest health food she'd found. Her idea of fashion was buying a new pair of Birkenstocks. Oh well, to each her own.

I walked down the sidewalk and past my store.

"Where are you going?" Alice asked as she matched my pace. "Is there a back entrance?"

"I have to see my friend next door," I said.

When I reached Heather's store, I pushed on the door. It didn't open. Below the MAGIC MARKETPLACE sign was a cardboard square that said BE BACK SOON. Heather's shop was on the ground floor of a mid-nineteenth-century brick building. Three additional businesses shared the space on the other floors. The inside of her place looked its age with original hardwood floors that had the dents and scratches to prove it. The walls were painted in a watered-down shade of chocolate, and mysterious-looking bottles of what I assumed were potions lined the shelves.

"Looks like your friend stood you up," Alice said.

Heather had a tendency to forget things if they weren't written down. She'd probably remember me soon and show up, so I decided to head back to my shop.

As I walked down the sidewalk, I dialed her number. The call went straight to her voice mail. Heather was constantly neglecting to charge her cell phone. Sometimes I wondered why she even had the thing. I opened the door to my shop and flipped the little sign in the window to OPEN. I'd planned on staying closed all day, but after what had happened, I needed to work to keep my mind off the tragedy I'd witnessed. Working with the vintage clothing always soothed me. I had a few recently acquired items to tag and place on the racks. While I waited on Heather to show up, I'd finish that project.

Alice followed me back to the counter. "This is a nice place. I love the lavender color of the walls."

"Thank you," I said as I placed my purse on the counter.

Wind Song jumped on the counter. She tapped my hand with her paw. I'd recently become friends with a long-haired white cat. After looking for her previous companion with no luck, I was starting to think we would be friends forever. This was no ordinary feline though. I had discovered her unusual talents purely by accident.

When Heather had discovered that the ghost of Charlotte Meadows had followed me home, she wanted to try out the Ouija board. Once Wind Song got near the thing, she'd started using her little paw to move the planchette. I know it sounds crazy, but that was exactly how it had happened. Heather took it one step further and brought the tarot cards. The cat actually pulled out cards that were relevant to the situation. I still hadn't figured out how she did it.

I took a can of food from under the counter and emptied it into the dish. Wind Song wasted little time chowing down. She was finicky though; she would only eat certain types of food. She'd even spelled out with the Ouija board that she hated the cheap stuff that I'd bought. So now I was buying the gourmet brand.

Alice bounced around the store, checking out all the items. "What are we doing now? Hey, are there any good places to go dancing? I'm really good at doing the Charleston."

My mouth dropped open. "You want to go dancing?"

"Yes, now that I have someone to talk to I figure we should have some fun. A girls' night out."

"I think I've had enough fun for one day. Maybe some other time," I said. "Plus, we're waiting for my friend Heather to get here, remember?"

Alice tried on a wide-brimmed hat and checked herself in the mirror. "Oh yes. Maybe she will want to have a girls' night out."

I stared at Alice. "Yeah, maybe."

Wind Song had finished the food and was licking her paws. As I placed the dish back under the counter, the bell over my door jingled. I popped up from behind the counter.

Heather confirmed my suspicions by saying, "I know, I know. I forgot to charge my phone again. Why are you looking at me like that? It isn't that big of a deal. You know I always forget to charge my phone."

Heather wore designer jeans today with a white peasant blouse. She had on brown flip-flops with big white flowers attached to the top. Her bangs were pulled back with a large butterfly barrette, and the back of her blond-brown hair flowed past her shoulders. Gold bangles covered both of her wrists. Heather never wore much makeup, but she always had a natural glow. Today she had just a little pink lip gloss on her lips and maybe a dab of mascara. She looked as if she had been somewhere special. I'd have to find out more about that later.

I motioned with a tilt of my head toward Alice. Of course Heather couldn't see my ghostly companion. Despite the fact that Heather advertised psychic readings, she'd recently admitted that she had no sixth sense. All this time I thought she was the one who could talk to ghosts, but it turned out to be me.

"Charlotte's still here?" Heather scanned the room.

Charlotte Meadows still made appearances even after I'd found her murderer. I guess she just wasn't ready to move on yet. Now I had another ghost hanging around. Lucky me.

"No, it's not Charlotte," I said.

Heather's eyes widened.

"Is this your friend? She's pretty." Alice walked a circle around Heather.

I repeated the comment. At least Alice would be off to a good start with Heather by paying her compliments.

"You're not going to believe what happened today. You're going to regret not charging your phone."

Heather closed the distance between us. "You're starting to freak me out. What is going on?"

"Someone drowned at the film set," I said.

Heather's hand flew to her mouth. "Where? When?"

"You've scared the poor girl to death." Alice shrugged. "No pun intended."

"It happened at Fairtree Plantation."

"Tell me everything." Heather sat on the velvet settee beside the counter.

"It was Nicole Silver. She fell in the pond, I guess."

"What do you mean, you guess?" Heather asked.

Alice gestured. "Tell her what we really think happened."

"We don't know that for sure," I said.

Heather made a time-out signal with her hands. "Okay, who are you talking to? Nicole's spirit?"

I shook my head. "No, this is Alice."

Alice sat on the settee next to Heather, though, of course, Heather wasn't aware of her presence. "You know," Alice said, "I have a really good feeling about the two of you. I think we're all going to be great friends."

I sighed.

"Who is Alice?" Heather sat up a little straighter.

"Alice is a ghost who is attached to some of the clothing that I got for the movie. She's sitting next to you."

"Whoa." Heather jumped up and looked around. "This is crazy. It's just like with Charlotte."

"Who is Charlotte?" Alice asked as she played

with the cat. Wind Song apparently could see the ghost and enjoyed the game.

Heather watched as Wind Song batted at the air.

"All I know is I was looking around the plantation before I left the set. Preston and Nicole were arguing, and then a little later when I got to the pond, Nicole was floating on the top."

Alice placed a hand over her heart. "Such a tragedy."

"They were arguing?" Heather asked. "Oh, this will be in all the tabloids."

"Tell her the rest," Alice urged.

"Okay, I'm telling her. So now I have this other ghost." I pointed in Alice's direction. "Her name is Alice. She doesn't look her age though. She's pretty and dressed in an awesome outfit, I might add."

Alice laughed. "Why, thank you."

"Why is she here though?" Heather looked in Alice's direction.

I cast a glance at Alice. "That's a good question. Why are you here?"

"I want to help you find Nicole's killer."

"But you were around before Nicole was dead." I eyed Alice.

Alice fidgeted her hands.

"Oh, maybe she's one of those bad spirits who is just pretending to be nice. I should get one of my spell books and see if we can get rid of her," Heather said.

Alice frowned. "I am not one of those bad spirits." She placed her hands on her hips.

"Uh-oh, now you're making her upset. She said she is not bad."

Heather wasn't convinced. "Well, better safe than sorry."

Movement on my right caught my attention. "Oh no."

"Well, butter my butt and call me a biscuit, there's another ghost here. Cookie, is that any way to greet an old friend?" Charlotte Meadows asked.

Chapter 5

Cookie's Savvy Vintage Fashion Shopping Tips

*If you plan to wear your vintage garment,
make sure it's in good condition.
Delicate pieces probably aren't the best
choice for day-to-day wear.*

I motioned with a tilt of my head. "Charlotte is here."

Alice stared at Charlotte. "So you're the ghost I've heard so much about."

Charlotte had big ebony eyes and shoulder-length brown hair. Her makeup and hair were always flawless. Today she wore a floor-length tan jersey skirt, a loose white tank, and a black sash around her waist. Her shoes were tan-colored flats, and gold jewelry adorned her wrists and ears. Charlotte was every inch the fashionista.

Charlotte marched around to the front of the counter. "What in the Sam Hill is going on in this shop? I leave for a day and all heck breaks loose."

Wind Song meowed in agreement.

"There are too many ghosts in here now." I rubbed my temples.

"Oh, don't be ridiculous. There's only the two of us." Charlotte studied her red-polished fingernails.

"Exactly my point. There are two of you."

Alice and Charlotte looked at each other and shook their heads in unison.

"I'm not going anywhere, are you?" Charlotte asked Alice.

"No, I'm not leaving either," Alice said.

"What did they say?" Heather asked.

"For some reason neither one of them wants to go away."

Heather leaned back on the settee. "I guess they like you."

"How did I get so lucky," I said.

Alice folded her arms across her chest. "I can tell you that I don't want to be second ghost though."

Charlotte sniffed. "You're already second. There's nothing you can do about it. I was here first."

Alice sighed, but didn't respond. It was hard to argue with Charlotte's logic.

"There's room for both of us, right, Cookie?" Charlotte asked.

"Sure. Two is the same as one."

"I think you're being sarcastic," Alice said.

"Don't forget to show your Southern hospitality to ghosts too," Charlotte warned.

"That's true," Alice agreed.

I threw my hands up. "Too much talking."

Heather looked confused because she wasn't privy to the conversation. Wind Song pawed at Alice.

"What's wrong with the cat?" Heather asked.

"I think she likes the new ghost."

"Better than the old ghost." Heather grinned.

Charlotte scowled. "Don't you have a magic potion to stir?"

Somehow Heather and Charlotte argued, but Heather never heard most of Charlotte's quips because I didn't want to fuel their bickering by repeating them. Maybe Heather was more psychic than she realized.

Heather jumped from the settee. "Oh, we should use the Ouija board to see what Wind Song has to say about the new ghost."

"The new ghost has a name, young lady." Alice shook her finger.

"I don't think that's such a good idea," I called out after Heather.

Heather had already made it to the door before I'd finished the sentence.

"You girls are such fun," Alice said with smile.

"Cookie is a sweetheart," Charlotte said.

Okay, now they were making me feel guilty for wanting them to leave. It wasn't that I didn't like them. I didn't even know Alice, but it wasn't fun waking up to a ghost sitting on your bed demanding attention or trying to shower with a ghost standing outside the shower curtain yammering away.

Heather bounced back through the door with the Ouija board under her arm.

"Wait until you see this," Charlotte said to Alice.

Heather pulled out the Ouija board and placed the planchette on top. Wind Song pushed her way to a prime spot in front of the board.

"Look, she loves this thing," Heather said.

It did appear that the cat was looking forward to giving us a message.

"What do we ask her?" I moved closer to the board.

"How about asking if the new ghost is nice?" Heather said.

"It's Alice. And the new ghost is nice," she said in frustration.

"The ghost wants you to call her Alice," I said.

Heather looked in the general direction where Alice stood. "Right, Alice. Okay. Wind Song, what do you think of our new guest, Alice?"

Wind Song reached her paws forward and placed them on the planchette. Alice released a little gasp.

"I can't believe she is actually doing it," Alice said.

"It gets better." Charlotte motioned for Alice to watch more.

Wind Song slowly pushed the guide around the board until it finally came to rest on the letter *W.*

"W," Heather repeated out loud.

"We can read it, dear," Charlotte said.

As if adding *dear* on the end wouldn't upset

Heather as much. Good thing Heather hadn't heard the remark. Wind Song continued her mission of delivering a message to us. The next letter was an *A,* and then she followed that with a *T.* By the time she was finished, her first word was *Watch.*

Wind Song paused as if thinking carefully about her next word.

"*Watch,* what do you think that means? What does she want us to watch?" Heather pushed hair out of her eyes. "Maybe she wants you to watch Alice."

Charlotte shrugged as Alice released a sound of disapproval. Wind Song moved the planchette across the board again. The next words she spelled were *Out* and then *For.*

"Watch out for," Heather said almost under her breath.

"Watch out for what?" Alarm sounded in Alice's voice.

Wind Song didn't stop. She continued to move her paw around the wood. The next word was *The,* followed by *Water.*

"Watch out for the water," Heather said.

My eyes widened.

"Was that a warning about Nicole?" Alice asked.

"It's a little late for that," Charlotte said.

"How did you know about what happened to Nicole?" I asked.

Charlotte stood beside Alice. "I was eaves-dropping at the back of the store."

"Well, I should have known. Charlotte is right," I said. "It is a little late for that warning."

Now Heather would want to use the Ouija board all the time. I was trying to discourage that as much as possible. We stared at the cat, waiting for another message. When Wind Song hopped down and took her favorite spot in the sunshine by the window, I figured her communication for the day was over.

"I can't believe the cat used the Ouija board." Alice looked at the cat in admiration.

The bell over the door jingled, drawing our attention away from the board. The only problem was the door was always open before the bell actually made a noise. Now Detective Dylan Valentine was walking toward us. Had he heard any of the conversation? The board was still on the counter, and I didn't want him to see what we'd been doing. I grabbed a couple shirts I had in a stack nearby and tossed them over the board. My expression probably looked like the cat's when he'd eaten the canary.

Heather had the same look on her face. I supposed I could have just blamed the board on Heather. After all, it was hers.

"Hello, ladies, did I interrupt anything?" He glanced over at the cat.

I tried to look nonchalant. "No, we were just discussing what happened today."

He pushed the door shut behind him, and the bell rang again. "I was just coming by to check on you."

"How sweet is that?" Alice said.

"He is a doll," Charlotte offered her opinion as she inched closer to Dylan. She'd been known to pinch him in the rear end—without his knowledge, of course, but to my great embarrassment.

"Is everything okay?" I asked.

Dylan closed the distance between us. He stopped in front of the counter and looked over my shoulder toward the covered Ouija board. Nothing ever got past him.

"I swear he knows there's something hidden under the shirts," Charlotte said.

Well, that wasn't such a shock because I'd done a poor job of hiding the evidence. Dylan definitely acted suspicious.

"I'm afraid I have bad news," Dylan said. "I thought I'd tell you before you heard the rumor."

Charlotte laughed. "Yeah, right, he just wanted an excuse to see you."

If Charlotte wasn't careful, she would make me blush.

"What happened?" I asked.

Dylan's eyes saddened. "There were signs of trauma on Nicole's body. Specifically, her neck."

Heather gasped. "What does that mean?"

"Just as we thought, Cookie, it wasn't an accident," Alice said.

A lump formed in my throat, and a pit of fear opened in my stomach. Who would have killed Nicole? Sorrow had fallen over the room.

"Was it the boyfriend?" I asked.

Dylan shook his head. "I can't give any other

information, but I wanted to thank you for sharing what you knew earlier."

I swallowed. "Of course."

Dylan stepped to the side as if he wanted to get a better look at what was behind me. I moved to my left to block his view.

"If you're sure you're okay?" he asked again.

"Yes, yes. I'll be fine."

"Okay then, I'd better get back to the office. Call me if you think of anything else."

"You should think of something else even if you have to make it up." Alice eyed Dylan.

"I like the way you think," Charlotte said.

"It was nice seeing you again, Heather." Dylan smiled and then turned away toward the door.

I didn't blame him for being suspicious.

Chapter 6

*Charlotte's Handy-Dandy Tips
for Navigating the Afterlife*

*Find batteries.
As many batteries as you can find!
Gather energy from batteries
and other electronic devices.*

"I can't believe someone was murdered in Sugar Creek again. What is happening around this town?" Heather said.

Charlotte marched past us. "It's been fun, ladies, but I have a prior engagement."

"Where are you going?" I asked.

"Sorry, it's a secret," she said.

Heather looked at the door in an attempt to see which ghost I'd been talking to.

"Charlotte isn't sticking around," I said.

"She's leaving for good?" Heather asked with wide eyes.

I picked the shirts up off the Ouija board and

folded them. "No, she'll be back. She wouldn't say where she's going though."

Alice was wandering around the store looking at all the clothing.

"Too bad," Heather said as she grabbed the Ouija board and tucked it under her arm.

"I haven't figured out where she goes," I said, placing the shirts onto a display table.

"Did you ask her?" Heather said.

"Sure, but she just smiles and floats away."

Heather helped me straighten the shirts. "We still don't know what the new ghost wants."

"Alice, it's Alice. And I told you I just want to help Cookie."

I placed a shirt down on the counter. "There's more to it than just helping me, Alice."

Heather got the gist of the conversation. "Yes, there has to be more."

Alice strolled across the floor toward us. "If a ghost isn't prepared for her death, then maybe there are some things left unsaid." She studied my rack of sale items.

"So you're saying you have unfinished business?" I asked.

"That's usually why they hang around," Heather said. "It says that in all the books I've read."

"There's no book that can tell you what it's really like," Alice said without looking over at us.

"What's your unfinished business, Alice? Is it lost love?" I asked.

Heather pointed. "I bet that's it. It's almost always lost love."

Alice put her arms around herself, a lonely hug. "I had someone who was special to me and I never told him how I felt."

"So it is lost love?" I asked.

Heather jumped up. "I was right."

"This isn't a contest to see who's right," Alice said.

"Of course not," I said, then repeated for Heather's benefit, "It's not a contest to see who is right."

Heather backed off. "No, not a contest."

"Just remember one thing, Cookie, never lose your true love," she said, looking me in the eyes.

I laughed. "I don't have a true love to lose, Alice."

Heather snorted. "You got that right. The girl doesn't even date. Her idea of a night off is going to the local café for takeout and then home to look at magazines and write on her blog."

I frowned. "It's what I like to do."

"It would be a lot more fun if you had someone special to share it with." Heather folded her arms in front of her chest. Her bracelets jingled with the movement.

I busied myself sorting through the mail that I'd left on the counter.

"So you'll just have to help Alice find her true love," Heather said with a wave of her hand. The bracelets rattled even louder this time.

I shot Heather a glare.

She shrugged. "Maybe then the ghost will be able to move on."

"If it wouldn't be too much trouble," Alice said with a bat of her eyelashes.

Heather and Alice looked at me expectantly. It looked as if I was outnumbered.

"No, no problem at all," I said through gritted teeth.

Alice clapped her hands together. "Okay, we can go find him now."

"Whoa, I can't do that right now. I have to close up the shop and take the cat home. Plus, it's been a long day." I blew the hair out of my eyes.

Alice looked disappointed. "Of course. Yes, I understand."

If she was trying to make me feel bad, it wasn't going to work.

"Of course, in return I am going to help you solve the murder," she offered as an enticement.

"Why are you going to help me? I am not involved in this investigation. I don't have to solve the murder," I said.

Alice quirked an eyebrow. "You owe it to Nicole."

"How do you figure that?"

Alice crossed her arms in front of her chest. "Okay, then I owe it to her because she was wearing my dress."

"That's not a very good reason," I said. "And I repeat, I don't need to solve the murder. I've been there, done that, and don't want to do it again." I rubbed Wind Song's head as she purred.

Alice placed her hands on her hips. "I'm not leaving if you don't."

I stared at her. "You can't be serious."

"Dead serious." She smiled. "Pun intended."

"What did she say?" Heather asked.

"She said she wouldn't leave until I solve the murder."

Heather shook her head. "Well, you heard her. I guess you'll have to do it. You get a lot of stubborn ghosts."

"I'm not stubborn, just determined," Alice said.

"That means you're stubborn," I said.

Why should I risk getting involved? I knew why. Because I couldn't say no to someone in need. Alice looked at me like a lost puppy, and my heart said yes. Besides, I would want someone to do the same for me. But if we were going to solve the murder and find Alice's lost love, then we would have to get to work right away—without Detective Dylan Valentine finding out. I was yet again sticking my nose where it didn't belong. I hoped I didn't get in trouble.

"I'd better go. Call me later." Heather headed toward the door. "Bye, new ghost," she said as she walked out the door.

"Oh, she's just doing that on purpose." Alice scowled.

"Sometimes she forgets." I tried to make an excuse for Heather.

Alice grimaced. "Not this time."

As soon as I opened the carrier for Wind Song, she marched right in. This was the first cat I'd ever seen who willingly agreed to be in one of these things. Wind Song loved to travel though, and she knew this meant we were headed home. I grabbed my purse and the carrier.

"Where are we going?" Alice asked.

I placed the carrier on the floor and opened the front door. "I guess you're coming home with me."

Alice floated out the door. Great. Charlotte still popped in and out of my house too. It was a good thing they didn't need beds because I wouldn't have the room. I locked up and then placed Wind Song in the backseat of my car. Alice was already waiting in the passenger seat for me.

As I started the car and shifted into gear, Alice said, "I'm looking forward to solving this murder. We should talk with that boyfriend, Preston, first."

"I'm not sure how we will do that," I said.

Alice watched out the window at the green trees and historic houses as we passed by. "Oh, you'll figure out a way."

Within a few minutes, we arrived at my house. It was on the outskirts of town, but my backyard overlooked a new shopping-center parking lot. I had a small two-story white frame house. It had window boxes with red flowers and a couple trees in the front yard. Alice was waiting for me by the front door as I got Wind Song out from the backseat. I shoved my keys into the lock.

"That's a cute keychain," Alice said.

It had a pink flamingo on it. Very fifties kitschy. "Thanks."

I set my purse on the small table next to the front door and then let Wind Song out of her carrier. She raced across the floor and jumped up onto the sofa to take her spot on the back. She loved to stare at the birds from the front window.

"This is my place," I said with a wave of my hand.

Alice touched the upholstered chair and then moved over to the fireplace. "It's cozy."

"Maybe it's small, but it's plenty for just me."

My decor consisted of a lot of vintage items with a distinct fifties flair—no surprise there. A silver sunburst clock adorned the far living room wall. My cream-colored sofa was new, but I certainly had a large collection of vintage furnishings. A kitschy plaster peacock wall hanging was displayed opposite the sofa.

Alice followed me into the kitchen.

After the long day, I was starving. I decided to make tomato salad and lemon-baked salmon for dinner. Of course I had to bake cornbread too. That was part of my family tradition.

As I prepared my dinner, Alice sat at the kitchen table. "By the sound of the argument, I'd say that Preston was cheating on Nicole and she found out about it."

I sat down across from her with my plate. I took a bite of my food and swallowed. Then I said, "That's not much of a reason to kill her though."

Alice tapped her fingers on the table. "Some people don't need a lot of reason. Maybe there was more to the argument than we heard."

"That might be true, but I doubt there's a way for us to find out."

After finishing my meal, I rinsed off the dishes and placed them in the dishwasher.

"I have to do some work," I said as I walked into the living room. "You'll have to make yourself at home."

I pulled out my laptop and settled onto the chair by the fireplace to do a little writing on my blog. I usually posted several times a week. At Charlotte's urging, sometimes I included photos of the items I found or sightings of celebrities wearing vintage items. Charlotte had been sharing her marketing advice with me, and her tips were paying off with increased traffic to my site.

Alice paced back and forth across the living room floor as I tried to concentrate.

I looked up from the screen at her. "That's not exactly occupying yourself."

She shrugged. "I don't know what to do. Can't you keep me company?"

Releasing a sigh, I closed the laptop and pushed to my feet. It looked as if I wasn't going to get any work done. I was tired anyway.

I glanced at the sunburst clock on the wall. "It's getting late. I should go to bed."

I faked a yawn. I wasn't sure what Alice would do while I was sleeping, but I had to catch a few winks.

Once I entered my bedroom, Alice sat on the stool at my makeup counter. My room wasn't a refuge anymore since Alice and Charlotte had entered my life. I had found a delicate antique floral embroidered quilt to cover the bed, and romantic vintage lace curtains hung on the windows. I had an antique crystal vase on the nightstand that I kept filled with flowers. I'd bought them for myself. I grabbed pajamas from the drawer. It was pointless to ask Alice to leave the room while I changed, so I went into the bathroom. I needed my privacy.

"Of course we can talk to everyone on the set too," Alice said through the closed door.

"Alice, you do know it's time for sleep, right?" I opened the door and pointed my toothbrush at her.

She waved her hand. "Sure, sure, don't mind me, I'm just thinking out loud."

Yeah, I hoped she stopped soon. After turning off the bathroom light, I slipped into bed. Alice was still sitting on the stool. I felt her eyes on me.

"Of course I don't know if we'll be able to talk with that crazy woman Vera Lemon. I may have upset her just a teensy bit when I slapped the hat off her head."

I tried not to laugh, but a little snort slipped out. I didn't want to encourage Alice, but she talked and talked. At around midnight I dozed off while she was discussing recipes. She probably continued the entire time I was sleeping. As long as she was hanging around I would have to buy earplugs.

Chapter 7

❦

*Finding quality vintage garments
doesn't have to be difficult.
Things to check for: hand-sewn,
handset zippers or bound buttonholes.
These are just a few of the signs
of a well-made item.*

When the sun flooded my bedroom, I forced myself out of bed. I'd had nothing to drink the night before, but with Alice's nonstop yammering, I felt like I had a hangover. Once in front of my closet, I had to pick out my outfit for the day.

"You should wear the blue dress," Alice said from over my shoulder.

"I think I want to wear the yellow dress today." I pulled the hanger from the closet.

"No, you should definitely wear the blue one. It is a blue dress kind of day."

I sighed, placed the yellow dress back in the

closet, and then took the blue one from the rack. It wasn't that I didn't like the blue dress; it's just that I wasn't in the mood for it today. It had a cinched waist and white trim around the sweetheart neckline with a full swing skirt. I paired it with straw wedge heels and a matching purse. Looking in my full-length mirror, I decided the outfit worked okay.

"Don't forget the lipstick," Charlotte said from across the room.

I jumped and my purse fell to the ground.

"True. You never know who you might see," Alice said.

"Will you please stop doing that?" I said. "You nearly scared me to death."

"That's highly unlikely," Charlotte said.

Alice laughed. I felt a headache coming on. I picked up my purse from the floor. "Come on, ladies, I have to get to work."

"I call shotgun because I get car sick in the backseat," Charlotte said.

"That isn't possible," Alice said from over my shoulder. "See, this is exactly why I didn't want to be second ghost."

"It's like I told you, dear, you're already second. There's nothing you can do to change that now." Charlotte marched out ahead of us.

Alice sat in the backseat, next to Wind Song in her carrier, with her hands folded on her lap. If looks could zap Charlotte into the next dimension, she'd be out of here. On the ride to town Alice came around to talking with Charlotte though. Charlotte had a way about her that charmed everyone.

"Charlotte," Alice said, "You have to help me. I want Cookie to figure out who killed Nicole Silver."

"Oh, was her death a murder?" Charlotte asked.

"Definitely," Alice said.

"Cookie is good at talking with people. She'll say she doesn't want to do it, but if you push her she will. She just needs a little nudge, that's all," Charlotte said with a wink.

"I am so glad that you have me all figured out," I said.

Charlotte tapped her fingers against the leather seat. "It's the truth."

I pulled up in front of the shop, shoved the car into park, and got Wind Song from the backseat. Alice and Charlotte were still discussing the best ways for me to investigate the crime. I didn't wait for them as I headed inside. Right before I opened the door, I spotted Preston Hart walking down the sidewalk.

"There he is," Alice yelled from over my shoulder.

I had hoped she wouldn't see him.

"You have to go talk with him," she demanded.

"Put the cat inside and go talk to him before he gets away." Charlotte motioned with her hand.

It was two against one, and there was no way they'd stop harassing me if I didn't talk with the man. I was surprised that the film star was out walking around in Sugar Creek. Wasn't he worried about being recognized? A big, muscular man walked beside him. With his towering height and thick mane of dark hair flowing all the way to below his shoulders, he looked like Bigfoot.

Preston looked even more handsome in person. His hair was perfect, his skin was perfect, and his features were perfect. I couldn't spot a flaw anywhere. I guess that was why he was a celebrity. I got Wind Song out of her carrier, and she hopped up in the window as if she wanted to watch the scene unfold. Luckily for me, Preston was walking in the direction of my shop.

I wondered if Heather had opened yet. She usually got there later than I did though. I hurried down the sidewalk in the direction of the men. Alice and Charlotte walked beside me.

"Don't forget to ask him about the argument," Alice said.

"I can't do that," I said out of the corner of my mouth.

The man with Preston glared at me as I approached. He stepped in front of Preston. His actions took me off guard.

"Hello," I said. "I worked on the set of the movie with the costumes."

The man looked me up and down. His stare made me feel like running in the opposite direction.

"I just wanted to welcome you to Sugar Creek. My name is Cookie Chanel." I held out my hand.

"Are you serious? That's really your name?" Preston asked, stepping around the muscular man.

"I don't think I like this man," Charlotte said.

"Me either," Alice sized him up taking in every last detail of his appearance.

"Yes, that's my name. Well, it's Cassandra, but everyone calls me Cookie."

He raised a perfect eyebrow. "Sure."

"Anyway, I'm very sorry about Nicole. My condolences."

His expression changed. "We were engaged."

"Oh, I didn't know that."

"It will be hard to finish the movie without her."

"I can imagine. Will they give you some time before you have to be back on set?" I asked.

He shook his head. "Probably not much."

I thought back to when I saw Nicole in the water. It was a scene I wanted to erase from my mind.

Preston moved to step past me. "Well, we're getting coffee. It was nice meeting you."

"Try Glorious Grits down on Main Street. Their coffee's always fresh," I advised him.

"Is that it?" Alice asked. "Aren't you going to ask him more questions?"

"What else am I supposed to say?" I muttered, hoping Preston didn't hear me. "That conversation was awkward enough. I don't think I could have asked any more questions. Especially with that big ape hovering around him."

I went back to my shop. Heather's still wasn't open, so I'd have to tell her about my encounter with Preston later. She'd be sorry that she'd missed it. The air shifted as Alice and Charlotte moved around me. I could tell they were upset with the way I'd handled the interaction with Preston. I couldn't help it. They'd have to learn to deal with it. With any luck they'd give me the silent treatment all day. I glanced back and spotted Preston and his bodyguard walking toward the coffee shop. There was something odd about Preston, but I couldn't pinpoint it.

Charlotte shooed me away from her. "Don't just stand there. You should go back and talk with him."

"Don't you want to get coffee?" Alice said.

"No, not really." I started walking toward the café.

I knew I looked like a crazy woman talking to myself while I stood on the sidewalk since no one was around. I hoped that my odd behavior had gone unnoticed. The muscular man paused in front of the café, and I wondered if he would catch me staring at him. Without seeming to notice me, the man turned to his left.

He walked over to a black Mercedes parked at the curb, opened the door, and reached in. Preston was waiting by the coffee shop door, but not paying attention to what his companion was doing. He seemed to be studying the sign in the window that advertised a chicken barbecue at the local Methodist Church.

After a couple seconds, the man backed out of the car and closed the door. I watched as he joined Preston at the coffee shop. They talked for a moment without going inside. I thought maybe they were going to leave, but then they went into the shop. At least now I knew what car they were driving, although I guess that had little to do with anything. I could be on the lookout for them again though.

Just when I was ready to turn around and leave, I spotted something on the ground by the Mercedes. Alice and Charlotte must have noticed it at the same time.

"What is that?" Alice asked.

"It looks like a bag," Charlotte said. "Some kind of a blue duffel."

"Oh, you have to go check it out," Alice said.

She was awfully bold considering she wasn't the one who would get caught.

"Yes, you definitely have to get a closer look," Charlotte urged.

Normally I would have said no way, but something about the situation intrigued me. After crossing the street, I tried to act causal as I strolled down the sidewalk toward the abandoned bag. If I acted normal, no one would suspect I was up to something, right? Finally I made it to the black Mercedes. Now I had no idea what to do.

"Get the bag," Alice nudged.

"What if someone sees me?" I said out of the corner of my mouth.

Charlotte sighed. "No one is watching, just get it."

"What if there's something creepy in it?" I asked.

"What do you think it contains? A bunch of poisonous snakes?" Charlotte asked.

"Possibly."

Charlotte scanned the area. "The longer you stand here, the more likely it is that someone will see you. So just act causal and pick up the bag."

The ghosts were losing their patience with me.

"There's a fallen branch there by the tree. Pick that up and poke the bag with it. If there are snakes in there you'll know it," Alice said.

I released a deep breath. "Okay, I'll do it."

This seemed crazy. Then again, so was talking to ghosts. I reached down, grabbed the stick, and jabbed the bag. I jumped back just in case something came after me. Nothing moved or made a noise.

Charlotte looked smug. "See, I told you it was safe."

I glanced over my shoulder to make sure no one was coming. When I was reasonably confident, I reached down and grabbed the blue duffel. It probably just held some clothing, but I had to admit, I was interested in seeing the contents. I guess I was curious about who had killed Nicole, after all. If it contained harmless items, I could return it to Preston and talk to him some more. I wouldn't mind another close look at those incredible eyelashes.

"Unzip it and see what's inside," Charlotte said.

"This kind of gives me the creeps," I said. Nevertheless, I carried the bag toward my shop and set it down on the hood of my Buick.

"You can't let a little feeling like that stand in our way," Alice said.

No, of course not. She wasn't the one intercepting the bag.

As I stood there with my hand on the zipper, I knew that I shouldn't look through the duffel, but I had to make sure it belonged to Preston, right? I unzipped it and rummaged through the contents. There were a few self-portrait photos of Preston flexing his biceps. A few articles of clothing, like T-shirts and gym shorts, and some protein bars.

"It must be Preston's gym bag," I said.

The words had barely left my mouth when I saw the other item. It was a jewelry box.

"What's that?" Charlotte asked, standing on tiptoes to peer over my shoulder.

I opened the little black velvet box. The diamond ring was huge and sparkled more than I remembered. I'd seen the ring before, when it had been on Nicole's finger. At least I was pretty sure it was her engagement ring.

How had Preston gotten it back? Had she given it back during their fight? Had they broken up? Preston didn't mention it today. He had acted as if their engagement was still on when she'd been killed. Now that I had seen what was in the bag, I didn't know what to do with it. It contained the expensive ring, so I couldn't just put it back on the sidewalk next to the Mercedes.

"What do I do with it?" I asked.

"See if the car is unlocked," Charlotte said.

"It probably has an alarm." I walked over to the vehicle and peered in.

I couldn't tell if the doors were locked unless I tried to open one. I doubted that the man would leave the car unlocked. Sugar Creek seemed like a safe town until dead bodies started showing up. With my adrenaline high, I reached out and grabbed the handle. When I pulled the door, it opened and no alarm sounded. Whew.

"That was a touchy situation," Alice said.

"You're telling me."

I tossed the bag onto the seat and slammed the door shut. I couldn't believe Preston had been so careless with the ring. At least it was out of my hands now. Maybe I should have told him I'd found it and that his car was unlocked. Then again, I didn't want him to think I was a celebrity stalker. I'd just leave it where it was.

"Now we know that he doesn't really care about that ring," Charlotte said.

"That's true, or he would have taken better care of it," Alice added.

I thought back about meeting Nicole. She'd briefly stopped in the store with several other women the other day. One woman—I thought—was her agent, and the other was an assistant. I'd sold Nicole a Dior floor-length blue dress from the seventies that she said she might wear to the premiere of *Moonlight and Magnolias*. I'd been excited because that would have been great publicity for the shop. I wished I'd asked her more questions when I'd had the chance, but I hadn't wanted to bother her. I had wanted her experience in my shop to be a pleasant one so that she could tell others how much she liked it.

I slipped into my store and tucked my purse behind the counter. The ghosts walked in as though they owned the place.

"They were fighting," Alice said.

"Well, we already know that," I said as I turned on my computer.

"That just means he had the motive. I wonder why the police haven't arrested him already."

I straightened a pink Suzy Perette silk gown on its hanger. "I suppose they have their reasons."

Charlotte moved toward the front of the shop. "I suggest you find out what those reasons are." She waved and disappeared out the front door.

"Yes, that's exactly it. You have to call the handsome detective and ask him." Alice tapped her finger against the counter.

After flipping the sign to OPEN, I worked on changing the dress on the mannequin in the window. I'd decided on a summer picnic theme in both display areas. This one would be from the fifties and the other window would be from the seventies. My mother had found a pristine condition vintage wicker picnic basket, so I placed it in the window with a red-and-white checkered tablecloth. I also placed small bottles of Coca-Cola next to the basket. I dressed one of the mannequins in red-and-white-checked high-waist cotton capri pants with a white halter that had tiny red flower buttons on the front. The other mannequin wore a handmade blue-and-white polka-dot dress. The neck and hem had red ricrac trim.

Wind Song looked up at me.

"Do you like the dress I picked out for the window?" I asked her.

She meowed, so I took that as a yes.

"You didn't answer me," Alice said.

"That's because the answer is no. I can't ask the detective any questions."

"Can't or won't?" she said.

"Both," I said.

Alice's voice took on a wheedling tone. "I just want to help you and the dearly departed Nicole. She was wearing my dress, for heaven's sake. It's like fate that I should help solve her murder."

"You have a strange idea about fate," I said and returned to my work. After several hours, I'd redesigned the windows and placed recently acquired items on the shelves and racks. Only a few customers wandered in, looked around, and wandered out.

When five o'clock finally arrived, I was more than ready to head home. Alice was with me, of course, but Charlotte had disappeared again. Maybe someday she'd tell me where she was going all the time. It had only been a short time ago that she couldn't move away from me; now it seemed she could go where she wanted.

Chapter 8

*Charlotte's Handy-Dandy Tips
for Navigating the Afterlife*

*Walking through walls may be strange at first,
but it's a pretty nifty trick.*

I had a simple but tasty dinner of breaded baked chicken and sautéed greens. Alice was pacing the living room floor, but at least she was being quiet. I welcomed the chance to do a little work on my blog. Wind Song was sitting in her favorite spot on the back of the sofa again. Her eyes were closed, but I didn't think she was really sleeping.

After blogging about the fun of providing vintage items for the film, I closed my laptop and headed toward my bedroom. It was time to turn in for the night, and I was looking forward to the comfort of my bed. I'd almost made it to the room when my phone rang.

I raced back to the living room and grabbed my cell. I was expecting it to be either my mother or

Heather. They were the only people who called me at that time of the night. Why did Dylan pop into my mind? Of course it wouldn't be him calling me.

"Cookie?" the female voice asked when I answered.

"Yes?" I said.

I wasn't sure I recognized the woman.

"This is Shiloh Northcutt. I wanted to discuss returning the clothing when the movie wraps up. Can you meet me at the Plaza Hotel tomorrow morning at nine?"

"Sure, I can be there," I said.

"Great, I'll see you then. I'm on the fourth floor. Room 408." Shiloh hung up.

This would make Alice and Charlotte happy. I headed for bed, and Alice followed me into the room. This was becoming her routine. This time I was ready for her though. I'd purchased earplugs, which I hoped would drown out her incessant chatter enough for me to get some rest.

The next morning, after a much better night's sleep than my previous one, I dressed in a forties taffeta black skirt with a delicate red-and-white floral pattern. My white cotton blouse had a Peter Pan collar and tiny pearl buttons down the front. Red pumps completed my outfit. I grabbed a white purse and was ready for the meeting. I'd drop Wind Song off at the store and then go to the hotel from there. That meant that I would be opening the store a little later than usual.

While I drove, I called Heather and asked if she could open my shop for me. We often looked after each other's businesses.

"Are you kidding?" Heather had asked when I explained why I'd be delayed. "If you're meeting with Shiloh, I'm coming with you. I don't want to miss out on the action. We'll both open late."

Since I didn't want to disappoint Heather, I said, "I'm on my way to your house."

I was thankful that I would have another living person coming with me.

After dropping off Wind Song and picking up Heather, I drove us toward the hotel. Alice and Charlotte rode in the backseat. Heather simply wouldn't allow a ghost to call shotgun and make her sit in the backseat. There was something I wanted to ask Alice, so I figured what better time than when I had her in the car.

"Alice, you've never explained how you can move objects." Her image was still visible to me in the rearview mirror.

"I don't know, it just comes naturally. I think if you want it bad enough it will happen," she said.

I supposed that made sense.

Charlotte studied the scenery out the window. I knew she wasn't happy that she hadn't mastered that otherworldly talent yet.

The hotel was on the outer edge of town. It had a large lobby with several conference rooms on the first floor. Shiloh had said her room was on the fourth floor. So the four of us stepped on the elevator and headed for her room. I wondered what Alice and Charlotte would have done if the elevator had been full? Would they have floated up to the fourth floor? I wouldn't have been able to ask other passengers to move over because I had two ghosts that needed a ride.

We walked down the hallway and stopped in front of room 408. I knocked on the door.

"I hope she doesn't mind that I came along," Heather whispered.

"I'm sure she won't care," I said.

Movement sounded from the other side of the door. Shiloh opened the door wide. She looked at me and then over at Heather.

"Glad you could make it." She motioned for us to come inside.

"This is my friend Heather." I gestured.

"Nice to meet you." Shiloh didn't seem to care one way or the other if Heather was there. Shiloh wore beige dress slacks and a white blouse. Her hair fell to her shoulders in soft waves.

"I guess you can imagine that the set has been chaos since Nicole's death."

I could imagine. "It is terrible to lose her that way," I said.

"Ask her what she thinks happened," Alice pushed.

Shiloh sat in the brown leather chair by the window. "We have to postpone the movie for a few days while we figure out what to do."

"Well, that's not as long as I thought it would take," I said.

Shiloh scowled. "It's longer than I have. Time is money."

I glanced at Heather, but she didn't say anything.

"I don't like this woman," Charlotte said.

Charlotte probably said what Heather was thinking.

"Does this mean you'll need to keep my vintage costumes longer than we had planned?" I asked. "I'm afraid I would have to charge an extra fee for that."

"There's just a few more scenes with a couple more outfits and then I can return them," she said. "Just send your bill to the accounting department."

I wondered if I would get back the dress that Nicole had worn when she drowned. I guessed not—Dylan would have to keep it as evidence, right? At least I hoped so because I wasn't sure that I wanted it.

Shiloh's phone rang. She looked at the screen and then said, "If you'll excuse me, I need to take this call out in the hallway."

I nodded. "No problem."

When she left the room, Heather said, "Wow, she is a bit odd. She doesn't seem to care in the least that Nicole is dead."

"I'm just ready to get out of here," I said.

Charlotte walked around the room, taking in the items that Shiloh had sitting around. "I don't see anything unusual," she said.

"You need to ask a few questions while you're

here. Don't let this opportunity go to waste," Alice said.

The ghosts wanted me to ask questions, but they never gave suggestions on what those questions should be.

"As soon as she comes back, we are out of here," I said.

Heather agreed. "She gives me a creepy vibe."

When I glanced over at the other chair by the window, I noticed a dress. But not just any dress. I crossed the room and stepped closer. I was sure I recognized it. I hoped Shiloh didn't come back in the room and catch me looking at her stuff. I reached down and picked up the blue dress. I knew I recognized it. I never forgot a piece of vintage fashion. Especially one that I had sold.

It was the Dior dress that I had sold to Nicole. The one she had said she might wear to the premiere.

"What is it?" Heather asked.

"This is Nicole's dress. I sold it to her the other day before I was on the set." I studied the blue fabric.

Heather and the ghosts stepped closer to me so that they could get a better look at the dress.

"It's pretty. She would have looked great in it," Charlotte said.

"How did it get in Shiloh's room since I had just sold it to Nicole right before her murder?" I asked.

"Maybe Nicole decided she didn't want it after all and she gave it to Shiloh?" Heather asked.

I frowned. "Perhaps, but she really seemed to love it. She even tried it on and it fit her perfectly."

"Everything fit her perfectly. She was like a model," Alice said.

I placed the dress back on the chair when I thought I heard Shiloh coming back. It must have been someone walking down the hall because she didn't enter and the footsteps continued past the door. My heart was in my throat. Snooping around made me nervous.

"I remember that day on the set, I saw Nicole show the dress to another woman. I didn't hear what they were saying, but once she was done she placed the dress on top of her purse and other belongings. I had to leave the area after that so I don't know what happened to it then."

"Maybe Shiloh is a kleptomaniac and she had to have that blue dress," Charlotte said without cracking a smile.

"I doubt that she is a klepto, Charlotte," I said.

"I can't believe I agree with her, but Charlotte may have a point." Heather was getting good at inferring what the ghosts said, based on my answers to them.

Charlotte placed her hands on her hips. "Honey, you should agree with me more often. I'm always right. And when I'm wrong, I'm right."

Alice chuckled.

"Okay, so anything is possible, but I doubt that. Shiloh had a lot of clothing from me and she could have kept any number of the items."

"You don't have the stuff back yet, how do you

know that she hasn't kept some things?" Heather said.

"True. And she does have the dress. So why would she steal it?"

Heather shrugged. "Maybe she simply liked it."

"Well, one thing is for sure. This definitely adds Shiloh to the suspects list," I said.

We were all huddled around that chair when Shiloh came back into the room. When I heard the door, I turned around. Heather and I looked in her direction. We probably looked guilty of something. I take that back—I knew we looked guilty of something. Shiloh quirked an eyebrow at us, but she didn't ask what we were doing.

"We were just looking out the window." I pointed.

"Beautiful room," Heather added as if we had scripted what we would say.

Shiloh waved her hand. "I hadn't noticed. So anyway, I will have someone deliver the clothing to your shop in about a week."

I breathed easier. "Sure, that will be fine."

She could have just given me that information over the phone. I wasn't sure why I'd had to make a special trip to the hotel to see her. But at least I'd seen the blue dress. Heather and I made our way toward the door.

"Thanks, again," I said as I looked back.

Shiloh was already looking at her iPad. "Yeah, thanks," she said without looking up.

"That is one rude woman," Charlotte said.

"I would never treat anyone so ungraciously," Alice said.

As we walked down the hallway, I asked, "Do you think I should have asked about the dress?"

"Definitely," they all said in unison.

"I guess it's too late now. Maybe I'll get a chance to talk with her again."

"That would be torturous, but I guess if you must," Charlotte said.

After driving back to town, I parked the car between my shop and Heather's.

"Thanks for going with me today."

"That's what friends are for," she said. "Besides, I wanted to get a look at Shiloh. She's just as unpleasant as you said she was."

I'd hoped I had been wrong about her, but clearly I was completely right.

After getting out of the car, Heather headed toward her shop. "I'll call you later."

Since I hadn't planned on being back at the shop until later, I decided to go to Glorious Grits for a bite to eat. I'd left a sign on my door that said I'd return at eleven. That would give me plenty of time to enjoy a meal at my friend's café.

Dixie Bryant and I had been friends for quite some time, and she was just like a sister to me. Plus, she made the best apple pie in the state, maybe even in the whole country. It was almost better than my granny's, although I would have never told her that. Signs with cutesy sayings like "Kiss My Grits" adorned the walls. Red-and-white checkered fabric covered the tables. Red leather booths lined the walls, with table and chairs in the middle of the room.

Dixie waved at me when I stepped into the café. She was a petite brunette with more energy than a hummingbird. She wore her usual uniform of white shirt, polka-dot apron, and jeans. The café was crowded, and I didn't see any empty seats in the place.

Dixie had a pot of coffee in one hand and plates in the other. It seemed as if she always had a pot of coffee in her hand.

"Hey, Cookie, are you ready for something good to eat? We have a lot of homemade specials today." She peered at me through her oversized white-rimmed glasses.

"You know I always am," I said with a smile. "It looks like I might have to wait for a table for a while. It's jam-packed in here."

"You can sit with me," the male voice sounded from behind me and to my right.

Chapter 9

Cookie's Savvy Vintage Fashion Shopping Tips

❧

*Measurements you should take
before your shopping trip are bust, waist,
hips, sleeve length, and shoulder width.*

I turned around to see Detective Dylan Valentine sitting by himself at a booth in the corner by the window.

"No need for you to wait for a table when I have all this room." He gestured to the seat across from him. "I just got here and haven't even ordered."

I was hoping that my cheeks hadn't turned red. I hadn't expected to have breakfast with Dylan.

Out of habit, Dixie grabbed a menu. "You'd better sit there or there's no telling how long you'll have to wait." Dixie placed the menu on the table and poured us each a cup of steaming coffee. "I'll be back in a bit to get both your orders."

I'd told Dixie about having Charlotte's ghost

hanging around, but she didn't know about my latest spectral attachment. The two were standing right beside me next to the table. I was determined to ignore them right now though. I couldn't risk accidentally answering one of them in front of Dylan. He would think I was crazy.

I slipped into the booth across from Dylan. He wore a white shirt and blue tie with black pants. I'd sold him a vintage outfit during the last investigation. It made my heart go pitter-patter just thinking of him wearing the clothing.

"So what are you having today?" he asked with a smile.

I grinned and looked over the menu, although I had the thing memorized by now. It hadn't changed much over the years. But why mess with perfection, right?

"I think I'll have the French toast," I said.

He placed his menu down. "That sounds good. I think I'll have the same. So what are you up to this morning?"

I took a sip of coffee. "I've just been talking with Shiloh about getting my vintage items back."

He took a drink of coffee. I noticed that he drank it black. Probably a cop thing, I figured. This was my chance to ask about the dress Nicole had been wearing.

"I guess the garment Nicole was wearing will be evidence?"

He stared at me and chuckled. "Do you want it back?"

My eyes widened. "No, not really."

He laughed. "I didn't think so, but yes, it is evidence."

Dixie returned. We placed our orders, and she winked at me as she removed the menus from the table. I tapped my fingers against the table. "So are you going to share any more info with me?"

A smile spread across his face. "Nothing to share, really."

I watched him to see if he was holding something back, but his poker face revealed nothing.

"Honest," he said.

"Okay, I believe you. How's that outfit I sold you working out? You probably need to stop in for a few more items, right?"

Had I really just invited him to the store? Why had I done that?

He chuckled. "The outfit is good. As a matter of fact, I do want to get a few more things."

"Well, stop by any time," I said.

"I'll do that." He took a drink of his coffee and then said, "If you'll excuse me, I need to make a phone call before the food arrives."

"Sure." I pulled out my phone to check messages.

When he walked away, Charlotte appeared with Alice. I knew they'd been beside me the whole time, but I'd chosen to ignore them. It was the first time I'd done that successfully, so I was a little proud of myself. Maybe I was getting better at this communicating-with-the-dead stuff.

"This is just the sweetest thing. A date with the handsome Dylan Valentine," Charlotte said.

"It is lovely," Alice added.

"It isn't a date," I said. "Just two people enjoying a meal together."

"One of which just happens to be very handsome," Alice added.

Charlotte laughed.

"Be quiet, you two, he's coming back," I whispered.

"Don't forget to put more lipstick on after you eat," Charlotte warned.

Charlotte was full of dating suggestions. I wasn't sure it was good advice, but I listened nonetheless. Dylan slipped into the booth across from me, just as Dixie arrived with the food. She placed the plates down in front of us. Then she set the syrup in the middle.

"Can I get you all anything else? Ready for more coffee?"

"No, I think we're good. Do you need anything, Cookie?" he asked.

Hearing my name roll off his tongue was a good thing.

"I'm fine, thank you."

Dixie winked at me again. "I'll be back in a bit."

Dylan sank his fork into the golden fried bread. "So, how's everything at the shop?"

I poured syrup over my toast. "Steady business, so that's a good thing."

He took a bite and nodded.

"Ask him about the crime, for heaven's sake." Charlotte nudged.

Ignoring Charlotte and Alice, I asked, "I never knew why you picked Sugar Creek as your new home."

"The department had an opening, so I applied. When I saw how nice the town was, I knew I would enjoy living here. I like it more now." He stared at me.

I blushed and looked down at my plate.

He continued, "I moved here from Atlanta."

I looked up at him. "I lived in Atlanta too."

"Really? What did you do there?"

"I worked at Saks Fifth Avenue as a buyer, but then I decided to follow my dream and came back to Sugar Creek to open my shop."

"I'm glad you did," he said.

"Oh, he is so sweet," Alice said from over Dylan's shoulder.

She was standing behind him now. Charlotte was hovering over my shoulder. Dylan and I chatted about Sugar Creek and living in Atlanta while we finished the meal. But apparently, by the frowns on Alice and Charlotte's faces, I hadn't asked enough about the case. I didn't want to push him for details when I knew he couldn't share them with me.

Finally, I looked at my watch. "I guess I'd better get back and open the shop. I don't want to disappoint any customers looking for a Marilyn Monroe–style halter dress or a Humphrey Bogart–type trench coat."

He placed his napkin on the table. "Yes, I need to get to the office. Thanks for sharing the table with me, Cookie. I had a great time." He grabbed my ticket that Dixie had placed on the table. "It's on me."

I reached for the bill. "No, you don't have to do that."

"Let him pay, Cookie, you don't want to be rude," Charlotte said.

He looked at me with insistent eyes.

"Thank you," I said.

After he paid and we said good-bye, I waved to Dylan and headed toward my shop while he turned in the opposite direction. That was an unexpected twist to my morning plans. I'd never hear the end of it from Charlotte and Alice, though, because I hadn't asked the right questions. At least they seemed tickled that I'd spent some time with Dylan.

I wasn't sure what I would call it, but I wouldn't call it a date. A date was when he came to my house and picked me up and we went to the movies, right? That hadn't happened . . . yet.

Chapter 10

Charlotte's Handy-Dandy Tips
for Navigating the Afterlife

Careful when scaring the living.
They may try to cleanse the space,
and then you'll have to leave.

The next day, after a restless night of listening to Alice complain that I wasn't doing enough to find the killer, I came up with a plan to go back to the scene of the crime. That was something I knew Dylan would probably frown upon, but the police didn't need to know. I wasn't sure if it would do any good or if I would learn anything new, but I felt it would be good to go back and see the area.

Maybe it would spark a thought that I'd forgotten. Plus, it would get the ghosts to stop complaining for a little while. I was missing a lot of sleep because of the nonstop chattering. Charlotte had even started to chime in now. So with both women in the car, I headed toward Fairtree Plantation.

The top was down on the Buick, and the sky was an endless blue. Of course it was already hot, but that was a given in Georgia at this time of year. The movie was still on hold, but the plantation was open for people to view the grounds until they started filming again. I parked the car in the lot.

"Don't make the mistake of walking on Vera Lemon's property," Alice said.

"What is that all about?" Charlotte asked.

I explained how Vera had gotten her bloomers in a bunch about people stepping on her grass.

"Oh, for heaven's sakes. That is just nonsense," Charlotte said.

All the same, I would try my best to stay away from Vera. As I made my way across the beautiful landscape, I was pretty sure I shouldn't be there, but I couldn't let a little detail like that stop me. After all, it wasn't like they'd banned anyone from the property. Not yet.

When I reached the pond, I paused. The crime scene tape had been removed. The scene appeared as tranquil as if no one had died there just days ago. The lake's surface remained still, with sunshine sparkling like a chandelier across the top. It was a stark contrast to the ripples in the water caused when they'd brought Nicole out of the pond.

"That is where I saw her," I whispered as if I was supposed to be quiet.

"Why are you whispering?" Alice asked.

"I don't know. It seems like the right thing to do." I inched closer to the water.

I had to admit I was a little afraid to get too close. What if I actually fell in? I wasn't that great of a swimmer. I could probably get out in a pinch, but it wouldn't be pretty. I'd wanted to erase the scene from my mind, but here I was back again. That definitely wasn't going to make me forget. When I turned to leave, I spotted something shiny in the oleander bushes up ahead.

"What is that?" I asked.

Charlotte and Alice peered across the lawn, but I knew they hadn't spotted the same gleaming item. I moved over to the shrub. When I peeked in, I spotted a cell phone. I reached down and picked it up.

"What did you find?" Alice asked as she leaned over my shoulder.

"Someone's cell phone," I said.

"That's odd," Charlotte said.

"The police couldn't have missed a clue like that," I said.

I looked back to gauge the distance between the water and the bush. It was probably about one hundred feet.

"It must have been lost recently," Charlotte added.

"Yes, it had to be. Dylan wouldn't have missed this." I pressed the button, and the phone turned on. "It's still charged."

"Maybe it belongs to another visitor," Alice said. "It probably has nothing to do with the murder."

"You're probably right," I said.

The phone lit up. I clicked a few buttons to check the ID.

"There's just one problem," I said.

"What's that?" Charlotte asked.

"The phone is Nicole's."

Charlotte's eyes widened, and Alice released a small gasp.

"How do you think it got there?" Alice asked.

"I don't know, but I still don't think the police would have missed it. And wouldn't the phone's battery have died by now?" I asked.

"How do you know it's hers?" Charlotte asked.

"It has her name and info saved in it."

Charlotte nodded. "That's a good sign that's it's hers, then."

"I don't know what to do with it," I said.

"That is quite the dilemma," Alice said.

I caught movement out of the corner of my eye.

"Someone is coming," I whispered.

I darted behind the nearest tree and pressed my body as close as possible to the trunk. My heart beat fast. Why was I worried? It was probably just some tourist. I was being too jumpy. But I was holding Nicole's phone in my hand. How would I explain that I'd found it? I would have to think of a good way to tell Dylan about this.

"Do you see anyone?" I whispered to the ghosts.

Alice rolled her eyes. "It's one of Sugar Creek's finest, sweetest residents walking around the area. None other than Vera the Lemon."

"You're kidding. What is she doing here?" I asked.

"I can't go ask her or I would," Charlotte said.

That was the bad part. It looked as if I was all alone out there. I needed to try to escape without her seeing me.

"I'm not on her land, am I?"

"No, far from it. But what is she doing here?" Alice asked.

"That's what I'd like to know," I said.

"I still can't believe she was so angry at you the other day," Charlotte said.

"What is she doing?" I whispered.

Alice and Charlotte watched from just beyond the tree. It was nice to have invisible spies. I didn't have to risk being caught because they could look for me.

"She's walking toward the pond," Alice said.

"I hope someone tells her to get lost," Charlotte said.

"She's down by the water now," Alice reported. "It looks like she is looking for something."

What would she be looking for down by the water? Then it hit me, "What if Nicole had gone to Vera's property and she caught her, then pushed her in the water?"

"That seems a bit extreme, don't you think?" Charlotte said.

"You saw the way she acted the other day," I said. "She wasn't being rational."

"Nothing would surprise me," Alice said.

"Where is she now?" My back was still pressed against the tree trunk.

I felt the bark through the thin cotton of my shirt.

"She went down the path, past the pond," Alice said as she stood guard.

This was entirely too sticky of a situation. The last thing I wanted was another confrontation with Vera.

"I need to get out of here before she catches me." Maybe she would push me into the pond too. I ran across the lawn toward the parking lot, praying I wouldn't fall flat on my face wearing my wedge heels. Every few seconds, I glanced back to see if Vera had spotted me. The ghosts had left me behind and were already inside the car. I supposed I didn't run fast enough to suit them.

Releasing a breath of relief when I made it back to the car, I jumped in and cranked the engine. Thank goodness we had gotten out of there before I'd been caught. Plus, I hadn't left empty-handed either. I had Nicole's phone.

Chapter 11

Cookie's Savvy Vintage Fashion Shopping Tips

*If you find favorite thrift shops,
make sure to check back frequently,
as their inventory changes often.*

We were headed back to my shop. I soaked in the sunshine and the slight summer breeze while listening to one of my favorite fifties songs, "In the Still of the Night."

"That's a romantic date song," Alice said from the backseat.

Charlotte was sitting in her usual spot in the front seat. Maybe Alice had stopped fighting for that prime real estate.

"Yes, it sure is—now we just need to get her another date."

"There was no first date," I reminded my ghostly companions.

"Whatever you say," Alice said.

Charlotte laughed.

They'd never stop talking about my breakfast with Dylan. The fact of the matter was it wasn't a date. After parking the car, I headed straight for Heather's. Unfortunately, she'd left a sign on her door that she'd be back in a few minutes. So I turned and headed back to my shop.

Once inside, I greeted Wind Song and petted her head. Sitting behind the counter, I pulled out the phone I'd found from my purse. I scrolled through a few items in her call history, and then I searched through her recently viewed web browsing. There was nothing much there other than celebrity tabloid Web sites and some clothing Web sites. I opened the screen for the text messages. That was when I gasped.

"This was definitely Nicole's phone, no doubt about it," I said, mostly to myself.

"What's wrong? You look like you saw a ghost." Alice snickered.

"This is serious," I said.

"Let me see." Charlotte leaned in closer.

"There are messages from Jessica Duncan on here." I pointed at the phone.

"And you're sure that it's Nicole's phone?" Charlotte placed her hands on her hips.

I scrolled back to the ID page and tapped the screen with my finger. "See, right here is her name and info."

"So what's the big deal about the messages from Jessica Duncan?" Charlotte asked. "After all, they were both acting in the same film."

I glanced over at her. "Well, I don't know for

sure. I haven't read them yet. I just saw the one sentence."

"That's not much to go on," Charlotte said.

"What does the sentence say?" Alice asked.

I looked down at the screen. "'Don't threaten me.' That was the response from Nicole to Jessica."

"Okay, I'll admit that does sound suspicious," Charlotte said.

"More than a little," I said.

"Read the rest of the conversation." Alice stepped to my left so she could look at the phone too.

I scrolled back through the messages. "It appears that Jessica accused Nicole of stealing the lead role from her."

"That's very interesting," Alice said.

I thought back to my conversation with Jessica. She hadn't seemed upset or broken up about Nicole's death. All she mentioned was that Nicole had gotten the part she wanted for herself. Obviously, she was not happy with the way things had turned out.

Why was the phone left by the oleander bushes? The killer couldn't have left it there because surely he—or she—would have deleted those incriminating messages. I'd like to think a smart person would have done that, but a killer couldn't be too smart or they'd never kill anyone in the first place, right?

"What else does it say?" Charlotte pointed at the phone.

I scrolled back a little more. "They were supposed to meet." My eyes widened as I read.

"When?" Alice asked. "This could be a huge clue."

"Right before the murder happened."

"She could've left the argument with Preston and met with Jessica . . ."

"And then Jessica strangled her and pushed her in the water," I finished Alice's sentence.

"You have to tell Dylan about what you found."

"I can't tell him. Not yet anyway. Not until I can figure out a way to explain why I was there."

That night I didn't sleep much. My new earplugs did a good job of blocking out the ghosts' chatter, but my mind was restless. I had to figure out how to tell Dylan about finding Nicole's phone.

As the sun rose on another bright, cloudless summer day, I forced myself out of bed and I picked out my outfit. It was a 1950s two-piece cotton play set consisting of a white cotton blouse and high-waist yellow-and-white-striped capri pants. The top buttoned up the back with small white buttons. My purse was a yellow-and-white polka clutch. I finished the outfit with white flats. Just because I hadn't slept well the night before was no excuse for not looking my best. I was my store's advertising. That meant always dressing the part.

After my morning routine of looking in the paper for estate sales and munching on Greek yogurt topped with granola, I gathered up my ghosts and the cat and headed to work. Alice and Charlotte discussed the crime as I drove. I wasn't expecting to see Detective Dylan Valentine waiting by the front door for me when I pulled up to the shop.

"Look who it is." Alice pointed.

"I see who it is." I shifted the car into park and got out, not taking my eyes off Dylan. Why was he there? Then I remembered that I had invited him back to the store to pick up a new vintage outfit. I hadn't expected him to take me up on that offer.

"Good morning, Dylan." I carried the cat's carrier to the door.

"Good morning, Cookie." He glanced up at the blue sky and then smiled. "I hope I'm not too early."

"No, not at all. It always makes a business owner happy to see a customer waiting for the store to open."

I unlocked the door and motioned for him to enter first. I flipped on the lights and let Wind Song out of her carrier.

"She really likes coming here, doesn't she?" Dylan reached down and stroked the cat.

She purred adoringly.

"Strangely, she does. She just showed up one day and made herself at home. It was as if she belonged here all along."

Wind Song popped up onto her favorite spot by the window.

"It looks like she does belong." Dylan smiled.

"I'm afraid I'm not here for strictly shopping reasons."

"Of course he's not here for shopping. Anything he says is just an excuse to see you, Cookie. He's going to ask her out," Alice said to Charlotte.

"It's about time. I've seen comatose turtles move faster," Charlotte said.

I had to tune out their chatting. I was just glad that Dylan couldn't hear what they said.

"Is everything okay?" I asked.

I walked toward the counter, and Dylan followed me. Of course the ghosts trailed along too.

"Yes, everything is fine. I didn't want to worry you."

"Well, if he doesn't want to worry you, then he can hurry up and tell you what is wrong," Charlotte said.

Dylan leaned against the settee. "Preston is at the police station now. He's been there for quite some time. The other officers are questioning him."

"Really? Why aren't you questioning him?" I asked.

"I was, but decided to let some of the others try. He wasn't telling me much. Just the same thing, that he didn't murder Nicole."

"So he's sticking to his story."

"But I really did come in to shop too."

My eyes widened. "You did?"

Charlotte stood beside Dylan. "No, he did not. He came in to see you. Don't be so naïve."

I wasn't being naïve, but I surely didn't want to

jump to conclusions either. If he said he wanted to shop, then that was what he wanted to do.

"What did you have in mind?" I asked.

"A date?" Alice answered for him.

"I need a shirt," he said.

"Okay, well, that's a start. What kind of shirt? Button-down, pullover, short sleeve or long sleeve?"

"I'd like a short sleeve button-down," he said.

"Nice choice. I'll see what I can find."

After gathering a few shirts, I handed them to him. He held each one up to his chest and looked in the mirror.

"What do you think?" I asked.

"I like your style. Which one do you think would look best on me?" he asked.

"Well, the blue matches your eyes. The green looks good with your complexion. And the white would go with everything. So honestly, I think they would all look great."

"Okay, then I'll take all of them." He handed the shirts back to me.

"I didn't say that to get you to buy all of them."

He laughed. "You're a great salesperson. You convinced me that I need them all."

"Yeah, sure," Charlotte said.

After ringing up the shirts, I handed Dylan the shopping bag with his purchase.

"Thanks for helping me pick out something."

"It's my job. Thank you for wanting them."

"Isn't this sweet?" Charlotte said.

"Look at the gleam in his eyes," Alice said.

If they didn't stop, I would definitely be blushing soon.

He held up the bag. "Well, thanks again. I guess my break is over. I should get back to the station."

I rearranged the jewelry on a rack by the counter. "Of course. Good luck with Preston."

I wasn't sure if I should thank him for sharing the info with me. Alice and Charlotte stood beside me as we watched Dylan walk out the door.

When he vanished from sight, Alice asked, "What do you think about Preston? Is the case solved?"

I shrugged. "That's a good question. I still would like to know more about the text messages from Jessica and why Shiloh had Nicole's dress. Plus, what was Vera looking for by the pond?"

"That's a lot of unanswered questions," Charlotte said.

"Are you going to tell Dylan about the phone?" Alice asked.

"Oh yes. The phone, I'd almost forgotten. I suppose I should. I just have to think of what to say."

I was still focused on the front door. More daydreaming than anything.

Heather opened the door and noticed me staring. "Were you expecting me?"

I chuckled. "No, I was zoning out. I just had a customer."

She quirked an eyebrow. "That's good. Is there something else you want to share?"

"The customer was Dylan."

"Ah-ha." She paused. "And what did he say?"

"He bought three shirts."

"I bet he didn't even need three shirts."

I shrugged. "Maybe not. But that's not all."

She motioned for me to continue. "What's the rest?"

"He said that they have Preston at the police station and he's being interrogated."

"Wow, so the case is solved."

"Not so fast," I said, pulling out Nicole's phone.

I shared with her my thoughts on Jessica and about seeing Vera at the plantation.

"Well, there's just one thing we should do," she said.

I eyed her suspiciously. "What's that?"

Heather pulled the tarot cards from her bag. "We need to ask the cat."

Ironically, Heather had found tarot cards that featured cats dressed in various costumes.

I shook my head. "No way."

"Are you still fighting me on this?" Heather asked.

"I'd like to see what the cat has to say," Alice said.

"I'm not fighting you. I just don't know about the information. Maybe the cat doesn't want to talk."

With that, Wind Song hopped down from the window and marched over to the counter.

"I guess that answers your question," Heather said.

Heather placed the cards on the counter. Wind

Song jumped up there and watched her as she spread them out.

"Okay, Wind Song, pick out the cards that you want," Heather said.

"I've got to see this." Alice stepped over for a closer view.

Wind Song reached out and moved a card and then another. When she stopped, she looked up at us.

"Are you done?" I asked as if she would respond.

Since she didn't pull out any more cards, I guessed that was her way of telling me she was finished.

"I can't wait to see what she said." Heather pushed a strand of hair behind her ear.

I was a little curious myself.

Heather flipped over the first card. "It's the king of cups card. This one means that someone new is about to come into your life."

I tried to look skeptical. "Interesting, but that could just mean a customer."

Heather shrugged. "I suppose. But Wind Song knows the difference between a customer and someone who is here for a different reason."

I just hoped that reason would be a good one. I never knew with the way things had been going in Sugar Creek lately.

Heather flipped over the next card. "This one is the high priestess card. It means that you shouldn't give up on your current mission."

"I don't think I could even if I wanted to," I said.

Just then the bell on the door jingled, and we all looked up as if we'd been caught doing something that we shouldn't.

Heather grabbed the cards. Wind Song meowed as she jumped down from the counter. It was just a customer. And that was probably who Wind Song had seen as the stranger coming into my life. The man probably wondered why we were staring at him. He wore a gray suit, black shoes, and a red tie. I had to admit he looked great in his clothing. The man had short blond hair and brown eyes. Dimples dotted each cheek.

"Well, hello, handsome," Charlotte said when she saw him walking my way. "You definitely need more customers like him. I wonder what he wants."

"He's a dreamboat," Alice said.

I had to admit he was easy on the eyes. Soon enough I would find out what he wanted. Maybe he just wanted to sell me life insurance or a set of knives.

When he reached the counter, he flashed that million-dollar smile again. "Are you the owner?"

I nodded. But for a moment didn't speak.

"Well, say something," Charlotte pushed.

Heather was staring at the man too.

"Yes, I'm the proprietor, buyer, salesclerk, book-keeper, and janitor." I stretched my hand toward him. "My name is Cassandra Chanel."

He glanced over at Heather and then back to me. "I'm looking for Cookie."

I blushed. "I'm Cookie. It's my nickname."

The dimples appeared on his cheeks again. I think the ghosts standing behind me swooned every time he did that.

"What can I do for you?" I asked.

"Make sure to sell him some shirts too," Charlotte said.

"My name is Ken Harrison." He shook my hand.

"May I help you find something?"

He pulled a card from his pocket and handed it to me.

"I'm a new attorney here in Sugar Creek."

"I had no idea there was such a handsome lawyer in Sugar Creek," Charlotte said. "He must be setting off a lot of talk in town."

His card matched what he'd just told me, but what did he want with me?

"How can I help you, Mr. Harrison?" I asked.

"I've been retained by Preston Hart."

My eyes widened.

"I wondered if I could ask you questions about what you saw the day of Miss Silver's death?"

"Has Preston been arrested for the murder?" I asked.

He shook his head. "He hired me and I got him out of there. The police were being relentless."

"Uh-oh," Charlotte said.

"I guess they were just doing their job," I said.

He looked me in the eyes. "Yes, I suppose they are. Anyway, is there anything you can tell me?"

I wasn't sure what info he wanted.

"I saw Nicole in the water, just before the director jumped in to pull her out. But before that, I did overhear Preston and Nicole arguing."

He seemed fascinated by what I said. "Is that right? What were they arguing about?"

"I couldn't tell you for sure. I think it was about Preston cheating," I said.

"What exactly did you hear them say?"

"I couldn't make it out clearly," I said, wanting to end the conversation. "Please excuse me, I have work to do here."

"You were at the filming of the movie all day, right?"

"Yes, I was there." Not knowing what to do, I busied myself by folding a shirt that didn't need to be folded.

"Was there tension between Preston and Nicole?"

I knew I couldn't avoid answering forever, so I finally said, "Not that I noticed, but they are actors, so how would I know for sure?"

"Would you call me if you think of anything else?"

I looked at the card again. "I'll make sure to contact you if I think of anything."

Ken looked around my shop. "You have a great store. I love vintage. Is that your car out there?"

I smiled. "Yes, it's my Buick. It used to belong to my grandfather."

"I've always wanted a car like that," he said.

"Maybe someday." He smiled again. "Anyway, you'll call me?"

I held up the card. "I have your number."

I'd almost forgotten that Heather was standing next to me. Ken smiled at her and walked out of the store. Wind Song watched him through the window.

"Well, I hadn't seen that one coming," I said.

"This is interesting. It sounds serious for Preston," Heather said.

"I'm not convinced now that he did it," Alice said.

"But you were so sure before," I said.

"That's before we found out all this other stuff."

She had a point. I was sure Preston had something to do with the murder at first too. Now I wasn't so sure.

Chapter 12

*Charlotte's Handy-Dandy Tips
for Navigating the Afterlife*

*Once you find someone who can see you,
stay with them.
It is a rare feat,
and you don't want to lose your new friend.*

That night I was trying to get much-needed sleep. But Alice just wouldn't stop chatting. At least when Charlotte was there the two of them entertained each other. But Charlotte had taken off again. My earplugs didn't protect me when Alice shook my arm and pulled the covers down from over my face.

"Cookie, are you awake?" she yelled.

"No," I said, giving up and removing the earplugs.

"Okay, well, there is just one thing I would like for you to do tomorrow. If you do this, I promise that I will stop talking so much."

I sat up. "Do you promise?"

She drew an imaginary "X" across her chest with her index finger. "Yes, I swear."

"If you'll let me sleep tonight, then first thing in the morning I will go wherever you want or do whatever you want."

"It's a deal," she said.

True to her word, Alice allowed me sleep. So the next morning, I slipped into a fifties-era vibrant watermelon-pink cotton halter sundress. The pleated bust had tiny rhinestone buttons, and the dropped waist had embroidered heart trim. My shoes were white sling-back kitten heels and my purse a white clutch.

"How do I look?" I gestured at my outfit.

"Fantastic. Now let's go."

Alice tapped her foot as she waited by the front door. I'd have to come back for Wind Song because I had no idea where Alice was taking me.

"Where are we going?" I asked as I started the car. In Charlotte's absence, Alice sat in the front passenger seat with the smug demeanor of a queen.

"I want you to visit an old friend for me."

"This should be interesting." I pulled out onto the street.

After she gave me the address, I pointed the Buick in that direction.

"Who's this friend?" I asked.

"His name is Bob Bowman. We were in love many years ago." Her voice was soft, as if the memories were overwhelming her. "He had a car just like this one."

"Really?" I glanced over at her as I steered.

She grinned. "I just want to give him a message."

"Is he married?" I asked.

"No, he is a widower."

"But you were married too?" I asked.

Alice nodded. "It just wasn't in the cards for Bob and me, but that's okay."

I hoped for her sake that I could find Bob.

After following Alice's directions for a few more minutes, I turned onto Rock Springs Drive and into a small subdivision. The entrance had a rock foundation on each side with ROCK SPRINGS written below.

"I hope this is the right place." I glanced at the houses lining the street.

"This is it," Alice said.

I counted down the houses until I found the sixth one down on the right. It was a brick ranch with green shutters and a small porch with two black lawn chairs on it.

"We're here!" Alice whispered.

Her voice was a mixture of excitement and nerves. I would feel the same way if I were her. Anxiety had taken hold of me, and this wasn't my long-lost love. I pulled up to the curb in front of the house.

I shifted the car into park. "Here I go."

Alice joined me as I climbed out from behind the wheel and walked up the driveway toward the door. I had no idea what I was going to say to this man. Alice had left that decision up to me. How would I explain that I had a message from Alice? What if he didn't remember her and Alice overheard that? She would be devastated. I didn't think I could handle Alice being sad. It would be heartbreaking.

I stepped up in front of the door and pushed the doorbell.

After a few seconds, footsteps sounded on the other side of the door. Then it opened. A man with dark brown hair, wearing a white T-shirt and blue shorts, stood in front of me. I knew this definitely wasn't the man Alice was talking about.

"Hello. Sorry to bother you. I am looking for Bob Bowman."

The man looked me up and down. "And who are you?"

"My name is Cookie." I paused. "My name is Cassandra Chanel."

"What business do you have with him?" The man scowled.

I hoped Bob was friendlier than this guy.

He inched the door closed a little more. "I'm his grandson and he doesn't know a Cassandra."

"I'm a friend of a friend," I said with a smile, hoping it would get me inside the house.

"He's not very friendly, is he?" Alice said. "Bob is nothing like his grandson."

I would hope not. It would be hard to explain that I needed to give his grandfather a message from a ghost, so I had no idea what to do next.

"My grandfather isn't seeing anyone right now."

"Well, I have a message from a friend. The friend is no longer alive." I rushed my words.

"That should work," Alice said.

"Like I said, he doesn't know a Cassandra and he isn't seeing anyone." He shut the door in my face.

That hadn't gone as I'd planned. How could I help Alice with her problem?

"It looks as if this isn't going to work, Alice. We'll have to think of something else," I said.

Alice seemed dejected. "At least you tried."

The sad look on her face made my stomach twist into a knot, but I couldn't do anything about it right now. We headed back to my car with our heads hung low. I climbed in and stared back at the house.

"If we only knew more about what Bob is doing. Is his grandson there all the time? If we can catch him home alone maybe he won't have a gate-keeper." I turned the key.

Alice sat in the front seat with her hands on her lap. She looked straight ahead at the street.

"Perhaps you can find a way to figure that out," she said.

I shifted the car into gear. "I'll see what I can do."

Honestly, I had no idea how I would ever accomplish that, but for Alice I would try.

The morning went by fairly quickly, and it was now after lunch. I'd picked up Wind Song and brought her to the store in time to work with quite a few customers. Business was definitely picking up. Maybe having Charlotte around was helping. She'd been giving me tips on effective advertising and merchandising.

I was at the counter tagging clothing when Heather bounced in, wearing a long flowered skirt and a Grateful Dead T-shirt with love beads. She was going for the Flower Power look today.

"I brought you chocolate," she said, holding up a bag. Ah, just what I needed, some peanut butter fudge from Sophie's Sweets down by courthouse square.

"How did you know?"

"I figured you had a busy day and could use a pick-me-up."

Business had picked up for Heather too. She'd recently been able to hire someone to work part-time and give her much-needed help. Wind Song jumped on the counter and placed a paw on Heather's hand.

"I think she wants to use the cards." I popped a piece of chocolate into my mouth.

Heather smiled. "This cat is awesome. I just happen to have the cards with me." She pulled them from her hobo bag.

"I had a feeling you might," I said.

Wind Song meowed as Heather placed the cards on the counter again. "I wonder what she'll have to say this time. She was right about the stranger last time," Heather said.

"Time will tell," I said.

Heather pushed the cards across the counter so

that Wind Song could pick out her selections. Before Wind Song had a chance to choose, the bell above the door jingled and we whipped our heads to see who had entered. My eyes widened when I saw Dylan. He'd caught us again. This was getting difficult to explain. Did he have my store under surveillance?

"Good afternoon, ladies. You look like you were caught with your hands in the cookie jar." He winked at me.

Alice laughed.

"We were just playing with the cat," I said.

Technically, that wasn't a lie. Just not the whole truth.

"How are you?" I surreptitiously shoved the cards toward Heather.

I knew Dylan wasn't back for more shirts. Wind Song was pawing at Heather's hand as she was trying to gather them up. Dylan looked over at the counter.

"Are you giving the cat a reading?" he asked Heather.

Heather smiled. "As a matter of fact, I was. You should come in and let me do a reading for you too."

The corner of his mouth twisted up into a grin. "Maybe I'll do that sometime."

Heather placed the cards back in her bag, and Wind Song jumped down. I'd have to give her an extra treat later.

"Did you come back for more shirts?" I asked, mainly to change the subject.

He chuckled. "No, I'm sorry. I love the shirts though."

So why was he here? Did he have more news about Preston? He stepped closer to the counter. Was he about to share confidential information?

Dylan ran his finger along the fabric of a shirt, as if he needed time to form the words in his mind. "A man was here to speak with you. His name is Ken Harrison."

I nodded. "Yes, he's the lawyer for Preston."

"That's him. So he came in to talk with you?" he asked.

"Yes, he was here."

Dylan looked concerned. Was I not supposed to talk with Harrison? I couldn't imagine why not. He'd seemed like a nice man, not to mention good-looking too. Not that I'd noticed much. Wow. Two gorgeous men in my shop in as many days. I was lucky.

"What did he say to you?" Dylan asked.

"He wanted to know what I saw on the morning Nicole was killed. I told him about the argument and then when I found Nicole at the pond. That was about it."

Of course that was all that I remembered. I didn't mention to Dylan and Ken that I'd picked up a ghost that day too. That wasn't as easy to explain as a simple argument.

"Did he ask any more questions?" Dylan studied my face.

I shook my head. "No, I can't think of anything else."

It was hard to remember every detail.

Dylan looked around and then met my gaze. "You know, you don't have to talk with him."

I waved my hand. "Sure, I know. But he seemed nice enough. He said he was new in town."

Dylan leaned his elbows on the counter. "He is. I don't know much about him."

Something told me that Dylan would be looking into him more now. He might feel as if the lawyer was messing with his case against Preston, but that was what he'd been hired to do. Ken wanted to clear his client as a suspect.

"If he comes back in, will you let me know?" Dylan asked.

"Of course," I said.

"This is getting interesting," Alice said as she eyed Dylan.

I couldn't help but glance at Alice. Dylan noticed my expression. He looked beside him and then over his shoulder.

"The cat was moving," I said, trying to explain away my odd behavior.

He nodded. Obviously, he believed my explanation.

"Thanks for the information, Cookie," he said.

"I want to help if I can."

Dylan smiled. "I appreciate that."

Dylan turned to walk out the door, but then looked down at Wind Song. She meowed at him.

He turned to face me once again. "Is there anything else you want to tell me?"

Was he talking about the cat and the tarot cards? Maybe I was just being paranoid.

"No. I can't think of anything else." I tried to act casual.

He looked at Heather, and she fiddled with her love beads. I knew she was thinking the same thing.

"I think he's onto you. Next thing he'll be suspicious of you talking to ghosts," Alice said.

I had a feeling he was already thinking I was a little off my rocker. Now was definitely not the time to tell him about the ghosts. I was glad that I hadn't mentioned the cat and the tarot cards or the Ouija board.

"The poor guy doesn't know what to think," Charlotte piped up behind me.

"Okay. I'll see you soon." He flashed his dazzling smile and walked out the door.

"That was an awkward exchange," Charlotte said. "You will have to tell him about the cat, and you'll have to tell him about us." She pointed at Alice.

"I can't tell him about any of that. No way. He'll think I'm crazy."

"You'd be surprised," Heather said. "People are a lot more accepting of the supernatural than you'd think."

"Maybe someday he'll find out, just not right now." I straightened the jewelry in the display case.

Charlotte shrugged. "You'll have to tell him sooner or later."

"I pick later," I said.

"I think you should talk to the lawyer again," Alice said.

"What for?" I asked.

"He probably has more information about the case."

I shut the display case. "I think the only info he has is from Preston."

"Well, Preston probably told him more than he would the police or you."

I picked up a pile of colorful silk scarves and refolded them. "His lawyer wouldn't share any of that info. It's confidential."

"I suppose you do have a point."

We stood in silence as we contemplated what to do next. There had to be a clue that I was missing. I needed to speak with Jessica about the text messages.

Heather must have read my mind. "You should speak with Jessica about the text messages." Maybe she really was psychic, after all.

"That's exactly what I was thinking."

"Great minds think alike," she said.

"Well, what are you all waiting for? Let's go talk to Jessica." Charlotte motioned toward the door.

"Not so fast," I said. "She's a star. I don't think we can just walk up and talk to her. She'll think I'm a crazy fan."

"You spoke with her once, right?" Heather

asked. "You could tell her you need to speak with her about the costumes."

Heather might be onto something. That might actually work.

"I just hope we're not way off base with this," I said.

Heather adjusted her bag's strap on her shoulder. "So what if we are? She wouldn't know why we are talking with her. The plan is just to be casual."

I put the scarves back under the counter. "I suppose you're right. I just hope it works."

Heather opened the door, jangling the bell. "Oh, of course it will work. What could possibly go wrong?"

Plenty could go wrong. I was willing to give it a try though. I didn't have any other ideas.

Chapter 13

Cookie's Savvy Vintage Fashion Shopping Tip

Remember to go off the beaten path.
You'd be surprised at the treasures you'll find
in out-of-the-way small shops.

The Gazette reported that the film's producers
had decided to continue shooting scenes that didn't
involve Nicole. So Heather and I devised a plan to
go back to the plantation and speak with Jessica
Duncan about her text messages to Nicole. I parked
the Buick in the lot, and we made our way across
the beautiful lawn toward the actors' trailers.

"I hope we don't run into Vera Lemon," I said.

"We'll just have to be firm with her," Heather
said.

I stepped over a thick electrical cable. "Yes, I
suppose that's the only thing to do."

"She can't say we're on her property now and
we'll just stay away from the edges."

Heather and I reached the area with the trailers.

Now we had to find out which one was Jessica's. The only way I'd gotten on set was because I'd kept the pass they'd given me. No one bothered to check it now. A blond muscular man who looked as if he might be a security guard was standing up ahead.

"It might be hard to get past him," Heather motioned with a tilt of her head.

"Just act like we're supposed to be here."

He was staring right at us, so I had to acknowledge him. I flashed the pass at him. "Here to see Jessica Duncan about wardrobe."

He motioned at the trailer next to us.

"Whew, that was brilliant." Heather hurried along beside me.

Once at the correct trailer, I climbed the metal steps leading to the door. My hand was frozen as I positioned it at the door to knock. Heather motioned for me to go ahead. Before I had a chance, the door flew open and I almost tumbled backward down the stairs. A dark-haired woman frowned and glanced back over her shoulder.

When she looked at me again, she asked, "What do you want?"

She blew the hair out of her eyes. The woman looked frazzled. I wondered if I had the wrong trailer, so I flashed my pass.

She glared at me and placed her hands on her hips. "Well?"

"I'm here to see Jessica Duncan," I mumbled.

She shook her head. "She's filming. She can't be bothered right now."

"Do you know how long she'll be?" I asked.

"Probably all day. When they're filming it takes a long time and she won't have time for an interview." She avoided my eye contact and studied her phone.

This woman must have thought I was with the press.

"I'm her assistant—can I help you with anything?"

"No, that's okay. I really need to speak with Jessica."

"Like I said, she will be a long time. She's taken over for Nicole since her passing and that means extra work for Jessica."

My eyes widened. "What do you mean?"

She sighed. "I mean that since Jessica and Nicole looked a lot alike then she will finish up Nicole's scenes."

So when Nicole died, that had given Jessica what she'd wanted. She would have the lead role now. Jessica would finish Nicole's part in the movie and be the star. Jessica wouldn't go to that extreme to get a movie role, would she? It was a competitive business, so I supposed it was possible.

"Anyway, like I said, she can't visit with the press or fans right now." She glanced down at Heather.

"Thank you," I managed to say before the assistant closed the door, ending our conversation. When I stepped down the stairs, the security guard was watching us. It was time for us to leave.

"He's staring at us," Heather whispered.

"Just act naturally," I said.

Heather glanced back at the trailer.

"Is she watching us too?" I asked.

"Yes, she's peeking out the little window watching us."

"We can't walk too fast or they will be suspicious."

"Right." Heather adjusted her hobo bag on her shoulder.

We strolled back across the lawn toward the parking lot. When I looked back, the assistant had reappeared outside the trailer but the guard had turned away. We'd almost made it back to my car when I spotted Vera marching toward us.

"Oh no. We almost made it out of here without being caught." I motioned toward Vera.

Heather sighed. "I can't believe this woman."

"Do you want me to scare her?" Charlotte asked, appearing out of the blue.

"No, that won't be necessary. We'll tell her we're leaving," I said.

For a woman who didn't want anyone on her property, she sure was on this property a lot. We hadn't gone anywhere near her land this time. Had she seen me here the other day too? Maybe she was coming to confront me about that. I would deny it.

"Ladies, wait for me. I'd like to speak with you." Vera picked up her pace.

"Is it just me or did she almost sound pleasant?" I asked.

Heather grinned. "She did sound chipper. Are you sure that's the same woman? Maybe she has an evil twin."

I laughed.

Vera reached us and thrust an envelope toward me. "This is for you."

"What is it, a court summons?" I asked.

Heather laughed.

The corner of Vera's mouth quivered. "No, of course not. Open the envelope." She gestured.

I still wasn't sure this wasn't a trick. I peeled back the envelope and pulled out the card. It was a cute green card with a watermelon slice on the front and a picture of a picnic basket. The words *You're Invited* were at the top. I glanced up at Vera, and she smiled. When I opened the card, I saw that I'd been invited to a picnic at her home this coming weekend. Why was she doing this?

"I do hope you can come. It will be fun. I've invited the film crew and they've agreed to come too."

Wow. I still wasn't convinced that this wasn't a trick.

Nevertheless I said, "I'll be there."

If the film crew was there, then I had to go. It would be my chance to speak with Jessica.

"Oh, and bring your friend too." Vera pointed at Heather.

I looked at Heather. "Sure, if she wants to come."

Heather offered a confused smile.

Vera nodded. "Okay. I'll see you there."

"Do I need to bring anything?" I asked.

It would have been rude if I hadn't volunteered.

"No, just bring your bodies." She chuckled, but that seemed forced.

Vera waved over her shoulder as she walked back toward her house.

"What do you think that is all about?" Heather asked.

I frowned. "I don't know, but something tells me we're about to find out."

Chapter 14

*Charlotte's Handy-Dandy Tips
for Navigating the Afterlife*

◈

*The living will try to ignore you,
but you have to be persistent.
If you focus your energy,
you can make your footsteps heard.
Moaning works too.*

Saturday arrived, and it was time for the picnic. I wore white capri pants and a pink-and-white halter top with wedge heels. As I drove to the outskirts of Sugar Creek, Alice and Charlotte giggled and gossiped in anticipation of spending the afternoon among the film crew. Heather couldn't make it because she'd promised to take her mother shopping.

Vera's home was also historic, but not nearly as large as Fairtree Plantation. It was a brick two story with a porch that spanned the entire front. As far as I knew, she lived by herself. I'd heard that she preferred it that way. The driveway was full of cars, and others had parked on the lawn. I was surprised that Vera had allowed that considering she didn't even want people to walk on her grass.

There were signs indicating that the party was in back. I followed the arrows around the house.

Vera had really outdone herself with the picnic. She had actually hired a caterer. Tables with white tablecloths and linen-covered chairs had been set up around the yard. A buffet table offered everything from hot dogs to ribs, potato salad, baked beans, and every imaginable dessert. BACKYARD TREATS was displayed on a sign in the middle of the table. My mouth watered.

"Stop looking at that food. You don't have time to eat right now," Charlotte said. "You have to look for Jessica first. You can eat after that."

Not listening to her orders, I grabbed a hot dog. "Just one."

Charlotte smirked. "A moment on the lips . . ."

I squirted mustard on the bun. "I've heard that before."

"Then you'd think you would learn," she said.

"I thought we were looking for Jessica," Alice said.

"I can look and eat at the same time." I took a bite.

I spotted Ken Harrison standing beside Preston Hart near a magnolia tree. Our eyes met, and he smiled. Seconds later, he had excused himself and was headed my way.

"Oh, here comes the good-looking lawyer," Alice said.

"I see that."

"Get rid of the hot dog," Charlotte advised.

"What am I supposed to do with it?"

"Stuff it in your mouth quick," Alice said.

"No way."

It was too late for that, anyway, because he was standing in front of me.

"What are you doing here?" Ken asked.

"What are *you* doing here?" I asked.

"I came with Preston." His smile was hypnotizing. "Are you enjoying yourself? How are the hot dogs?"

I gestured with my half-eaten snack. "Great. You should try one."

Charlotte groaned.

Ken grabbed a napkin from the table and reached out, touching my face with it. "You had a little mustard on your chin."

Heat rushed to my cheeks. "Thanks."

"I told you to get rid of that thing," Charlotte said.

"It's a beautiful day for a picnic." He gestured toward the blue sky.

"Yes, it is," I answered. "So, how are things going?"

He lifted a brow. "With?"

"The case against your client."

He laughed. "I'm surprised you're interested."

"Oh, I didn't mean anything by the question. I was just making conversation."

"You need to work on your detective skills." Charlotte shook her head.

"No, I know what you mean. The paparazzi have been around though." Ken grabbed a hot dog from the table. He slathered it with mustard, ketchup, and relish.

"Really? I haven't seen them, but then again I guess I haven't paid attention."

I'd been too worried about finding out who did this to Nicole to notice much else.

"The case against Preston is flimsy, at best. I'm working on finding out who really did this to Nicole."

My eyes widened. Charlotte and Alice perked up too.

"Do you have any clues or leads?"

He stared at me for a beat. "I might have a couple. You seem interested."

"Well, I am a little since I was the first one to see her in the water. You understand, right?" I asked.

"Oh sure, sure. I can understand that. I wish that hadn't happened to you." He took a bite of his hot dog.

"Thanks," I said.

"He sure is sweet," Alice said.

"Not bad looking either," Charlotte said.

They'd made their opinions known before so I didn't need a recap. Now I thought they were just trying to play cupid. Nevertheless, I needed to talk with Ken to find out what he knew about the investigation. He seemed friendly, but I wasn't sure how easy it would be to get info from him.

A man sitting with a group of other men called out to Ken.

"It looks like they need you." I pointed.

He held up his finger. "They're lawyers too. They work for the film studio."

"Well, I've kept you long enough. You should talk with them," I said.

So much for asking him questions now.

"I've enjoyed the company," he said.

I couldn't hold back a smile. "I'll see you around."

He smiled. "I hope so."

I watched as Ken walked across the lawn to the men sitting on the chairs. He sat next to them, then looked in my direction. Unfortunately, he caught me watching him.

"Ken sure is nice," Alice said.

"Yes, you said that a few times."

"I'm just saying. You should get to know him better."

"I thought you wanted me to talk with the detective."

"Oh, we want you to talk with him too. No need in putting all your eggs in one basket," Charlotte said.

I groaned. "You two need to stay out of my dating life."

"What dating life?" Charlotte asked.

"Good point," I said. "Anyway, I can't just stand

here." I finished off my hot dog. "I need to find Jessica."

As I scanned the crowd, I thought I spotted her next to the gazebo with a group of women. Two of the women—the one who looked like Jessica and another who looked like the assistant I met at her trailer—walked away from the group. Their backs were toward me, so I couldn't be sure it was them.

"I think Jessica went inside Vera's house," I said.

"Well, what are you waiting for?" Charlotte said.

"Let's go get her," Alice added.

"This makes me nervous," I said as I walked across the lawn toward Vera's.

Charlotte walked along beside me. "Vera can't expect guests not to use the restroom. That will be your excuse for going inside."

Charlotte had a point.

If I was caught, I would pretend to be looking for the ladies' room. Anyway, I hadn't spotted Vera yet. Part of me feared she was hiding somewhere watching everyone. Just waiting for her chance to scream for everyone to get off her land.

The back door was open with just the screen door stopping the bugs from finding their way inside. The hinge squeaked loudly when I opened it. Good thing everyone was talking loudly—I didn't think they'd heard me. The entrance led right into the spacious kitchen. The room looked as if it had been updated recently with maple cabinets and stainless steel appliances.

Making my way past the Viking range and Miele dishwasher, I stepped into a hallway. I could see quite a few doors leading off it. It would be easy to get lost in there.

"How do I know which room to look in?" I whispered.

Was I the only one in the house? Maybe Vera was inside.

Charlotte and Alice started poking their heads inside the closed doors.

"This is a closet," Charlotte reported.

"Laundry room," Alice said.

I continued my trek down the long hallway. Alice had floated all the way to the end.

"I bet the bathroom is here." She poked her head in. "Yep. Here it is."

I moved toward it, but before reaching the end of the hall, I looked to my right. That was when I saw a bedroom door partly open.

"I wonder what's in here," I whispered.

With any luck, I wouldn't discover Vera. Something told me she wouldn't be happy to find me poking around. I inched closer to the door. Looking around, I made sure no one was watching.

"Now you're making me nervous. I'm not going in until you look first," Charlotte said.

With a little nudge of my foot, I had a better view inside the room. An iron bed was covered with a blue-and-white quilt. An old trunk sat at its foot. Photos of Nicole Silver were all over the wall, as if Vera had used them as wallpaper.

"Whoa. What is going on in here?" Charlotte asked when she caught a glimpse.

"That's what I'd like to know," I said.

It looked as if Vera had been obsessed with the blond actress. I inched into the room. Just being in there gave me the creeps.

"This is bizarre," Alice said. "I knew that woman was crazy."

I had to admit this was the strangest thing I'd ever seen.

Charlotte motioned toward the door. "We should get out of here. If Vera finds out we've discovered her little shrine, she'll be most unhappy."

"Why did she leave the door open? She had to know someone might see it when they came inside looking for the powder room," I said.

"It was probably an accident and she didn't mean to leave it like that," Alice said.

I studied the wall. There were magazine clippings and even a professional headshot that had been signed by Nicole. "To my biggest fan, Vera," it read. I bet Nicole had no idea Vera had so many photos of her. The others looked as if they had been taken while on the set of the current movie.

My hand flew to my mouth. "Look at this shot."

Alice and Charlotte came closer.

"It's Nicole standing by the pond. That's my dress," Alice said. "The one she was wearing the day she was murdered."

"That means Vera had to be close to Nicole to

take this photo." Charlotte pointed out. "Maybe close enough to push her in the water."

I'd been thinking the same thing. The sound of footsteps grabbed my attention. It was definitely time for me to get out of there. Someone was coming down the hallway. I prayed that someone wasn't Vera. I rushed over to the door, but the noise was getting louder.

"Hide in the closet," Charlotte said.

"No way." I'd gotten enough of that during the last escapades with Charlotte. I paused by the door and then peeked out into the hallway. "No one is there."

"Maybe the place is haunted," Charlotte said.

I glared at her. "Very funny."

I stepped out into the hallway and hurried toward the kitchen. I'd almost made it to the door when I ran smack into someone's muscular chest. A groan escaped my lips.

"Are you okay?" Dylan asked, holding my upper arms to steady me.

I looked up at him. "I think so."

How had he known I was in the house?

"I thought I saw you here," he said.

"Yes, I was just looking for the restroom. It's a big house. Easy to get lost." I couldn't look him in the eye.

"It is a big house."

"So Vera invited you to the picnic?" I asked.

The corners of his mouth twisted up. "Does that surprise you?"

"No. I just meant . . . Well, I don't know what I

meant. I guess I didn't know she knew so many people."

"Vera knows everyone in town. And if she doesn't know you then she knows someone who knows you."

"So that means most of Sugar Creek is here," I said.

"Almost the whole town," he said.

"I didn't know she had that many friends."

"Vera doesn't make friends," he said.

"Then why do they come?"

"That's a good question. Just to be polite, I guess. Or out of curiosity."

I hoped that Dylan hadn't seen me snooping. But the worst part was I had to confess to him about what I'd found. I couldn't let this disturbing detail go without sharing it with him. Maybe he could confront Vera with this information.

Dylan looked at me. "Are you sick?"

"I wouldn't be surprised if you did get sick after eating that hot dog," Charlotte said.

I tried to ignore her lame attempt at wit. "As a matter of fact, there is something I need to show you."

He held me at arm's length. "Oh yeah? What's that?"

"I happened to notice something in one of the bedrooms on my way to the bathroom." Okay, I knew by his expression that he wasn't buying that excuse. At least I'd tried though. He couldn't prove that it hadn't happened that way.

"What are we looking at?" he asked.

I motioned for Dylan to follow me.

When I reached the room, I stopped. "I think you should see what's in here."

He stepped in front of me. "Okay. Let's have a look."

I stepped out of the way. Dylan moved into the room, and I followed him. It was just as creepy the second time as the first. He stood in the middle of the room, speechless, as he looked at the twisted shrine to Nicole Silver.

"I guess you can see why I thought you should have a look."

He ran his hand through his hair. "It's definitely strange."

"You can say that again," Charlotte said.

Alice stood in the hallway. She didn't even want to see it again.

"Why does she have this?" I asked. "I guess for the obvious reasons."

"She must be an obsessed fan. That doesn't necessarily mean that she wanted to harm Nicole," he said.

I wondered if he could be right. "No, of course not."

"But I'll look into it," he said.

"There was one more thing." I stepped closer to the wall. "This picture looks as if it was taken right before she was killed."

He moved in for a closer look. He probably hadn't been ready for that development. I felt that was fairly significant. At least now he could ask Vera questions about it. Footsteps sounded again.

Dylan probably saw the panic in my eyes. He placed his hand on the small of my back and guided me toward the door.

"Don't worry. If it's Vera, I will talk with her."

That was fine by me.

Dylan stuck his head out into the hallway. He motioned for me to follow him. Why did I keep hearing footsteps and no one was there? Maybe Charlotte was right about that haunted thing. We'd just stepped out into the hallway when the footsteps sounded again. Where were they coming from? It didn't sound like it was upstairs. That was when I realized someone must be in the kitchen. It was probably Vera, and we would have to talk with her. Would Dylan ask her about the pictures right there in front of me?

"Sounds like someone is in the kitchen." I swallowed hard.

"Don't worry." He grabbed my hand, catching me off guard.

With Dylan leading the way, we reached the kitchen. The screen door banged against the frame. Someone had been in the room. I looked down at Dylan's hand still wrapped around mine. He noticed and released his grip. Heat rushed to my cheeks.

"I thought for sure it was Vera," I whispered.

"I'll see if I can find her outside."

"I'd better get back out there. People will wonder where I went."

Okay, no one even knew I was here other than Ken Harrison. Dylan guided me toward the door again. We'd just stepped outside when his cell phone rang.

"Can you wait while I take this call?" he asked, moving a few feet away.

I paused. "Sure."

"What was that about back there?" Charlotte asked.

"What was what about?" I asked.

"He was holding your hand."

I waved off the question. "That was nothing."

I wondered if my cheeks were still blushing. Dylan clicked off his phone and stepped back over to me.

"I'm afraid I have to go. I'll have to talk with Vera later."

If he wasn't staying, then I wasn't staying either. I didn't want to encounter Vera by myself.

"I should go too," I said.

"Let me walk you to your car."

Dylan and I walked past the loud, lively party guests to the parking lot.

Stopping, he said, "I'll call you as soon as I talk with Vera."

"Sorry if it seems as if I was snooping," I said.

He smiled. "You're just a little curious, right?"

I grinned. "Yes, that's it . . . curious."

I climbed behind the wheel of my Buick. Dylan closed the door for me. "I'll talk to you soon."

"Yes, take care." I cranked the engine.

We watched as Dylan headed for his car.

"That was it? You had nothing else to say to

him?" Charlotte stared at me from the passenger seat.

"What else was I supposed to say?"

Charlotte didn't answer. I looked into the rearview mirror at Alice, and she just shrugged.

Shifting the car into gear, I said, "Anyway, I hope he finds out what is going on with Vera."

"I bet she is guilty," Alice said.

Alice thought everyone was guilty. But I had to agree—the photo collection was suspicious. I just hoped we found answers soon.

A murderer was out there and needed to be behind bars.

Chapter 15

Cookie's Savvy Vintage Fashion Shopping Tips

*Look through all the items in a shop.
Just because at first glance you don't see
what you're looking for doesn't mean you
won't find that diamond in the rough.*

The next day I stood in my shop with Charlotte and Alice beside me. I hadn't spoken with Dylan, so I assumed that he hadn't talked with Vera yet. Alice and Charlotte were anxiously waiting to hear from him. Okay, I was anxiously awaiting his phone call too.

Until then, the ghost gals were discussing all the clues we had to date. It seemed as if there were plenty of suspects who could have done harm to Nicole. If only I could rule someone out or narrow down the list of suspects. I had an idea though. Even I was surprised at myself for wanting to do this.

I picked up the phone and dialed. Heather answered on the first ring.

"Are you busy?" I asked.

"No, it's been dead all morning. What about you?"

I glanced at Charlotte and Alice. "Yeah, it's dead here too. Literally."

"Is there something you need?" she asked.

I released a deep breath and then said, "How about if you bring the Ouija board over here?"

"Are you serious?" Heather asked.

"I'm afraid I am."

"What changed your mind?"

"I guess I've run out of ideas. Plus, I'm curious as to what Wind Song will say."

"I thought you'd never ask."

Heather hung up the phone, and within a minute she was walking through the door with the board under her arm. She had a huge smile on her face.

"I've finally brought you around to my way of thinking," she said.

"That's a scary thought," Charlotte said.

Heather looked around the room. "If Charlotte's here, I know she had something snarky to say."

Charlotte and I laughed.

"Charlotte and Alice are both here."

Wind Song jumped from the window and up onto the counter. I didn't have to ask her to come over. She was more than ready. Heather set up the board and we watched as Wind Song moved closer. She stared at the board for a second, and I wondered if she was going to use it this time. Finally she reached out her paw and placed it on the planchette.

"This is amazing," Alice said.

I was still astonished, too, every time I saw Wind Song do this.

The cat started out slowly, just moving the indicator slightly. Then she picked up the pace, and I figured she was headed for a specific letter. Wind Song moved the planchette around the board and stopped on the letter *T.* Once again Heather read the letters out loud. When Wind Song was finished with the first word, she'd spelled out *tuna.*

The next word was *gourmet.* And finally, the last two words were *buy more.* That was the message the cat had for me? To buy more of her favorite cat food?

"Is that all you have to say, Wind Song? Isn't there anything else?"

She'd probably tell me to buy more treats next. I drew the line at getting her a mouse. I'd almost given up on Wind Song giving us any kind of significant message. But she did move the planchette again.

"Okay, I'll buy the food, Wind Song, now give us another message."

I felt ridiculous for asking the cat to give me a message about a murder investigation. Dylan would definitely think I'd lost my mind if he was witness to this. Wind Song moved the planchette around the board. The first letter was *J* and then *E.*

Next she moved it to the *S,* then pulled it away and moved it back to the *S* again.

"She spelled out *Jessica,*" Heather said.

"We saw it too," Charlotte said.

I couldn't believe it.

"What does that mean?" I asked.

"I don't know, but we should find out." Heather said.

"See, I knew Jessica was suspicious," Alice said.

"Alice, you're suspicious of everyone."

Alice smiled. "Maybe everyone pushed her in the water."

"Now that would have been something, but I highly doubt that happened."

Once the cat had shocked us with Jessica's name, she jumped down and went back to the sunshine.

"She really does get bored with us easily," Heather said.

"Well, she is a cat," I said.

"We should really look into this." Charlotte tapped her finger on the counter. "That is too much just to let it go."

I agreed. "Yes, I know we should look into it. But I don't know how. What do I say? The cat told me to question you?"

Heather shrugged. "You could try. You'll have to talk with her again."

"I can't tell Dylan about this. He's probably already questioned Jessica."

"The police only seem focused on Preston. They may be way off base," Charlotte said.

"Yes, they could be wrong," Alice said.

The bell over the door jingled, and I almost expected to see Dylan come through the door. He had a knack for catching us when we were using the Ouija board or the tarot cards. This time it was actually a customer.

Heather grabbed the board and stuck it under the counter. The shopper probably didn't want to see us doing some kind of black magic. I stepped around the counter and moved toward the woman who'd just entered.

"Hello, welcome to It's Vintage, Y'all. How can I help you?"

The blond woman asked for help finding a dress for a swing dance to be held at the Sugar Creek Country Club, so I left Heather with the ghosts. It was too bad she couldn't talk with them. Although Charlotte and Heather always had a banter going on through me, I had to deliver their messages.

I pulled out a few dresses for the lady, and she settled on two of them. It was always hard for me to let go of the pieces. But as long as I thought they were going to a good home, that made it easier. I hoped other ladies planning to attend the dance would also come to the shop for an outfit.

After ringing up the customer, I placed the dresses in a bag and handed it to the woman. "Thanks for shopping at It's Vintage, Y'all. Please come back."

"See, I told you my marketing skills would pay off." Charlotte held her chin up high.

I had to admit, business had been up since she'd

come into the picture. Maybe I hadn't thanked her enough.

"Thanks, Charlotte. You were right. That ad and the Web site have helped. I've even gotten more traffic to my blog."

Charlotte smiled. "What can I say? I know what I'm doing."

Heather grabbed the board from under the counter. "Are you sure you don't want me to leave this?"

I waved it away. "No, thanks. You can just bring it over sometimes, but just don't leave it."

At first I hadn't even wanted the thing in the store.

"Let me know when you're going to the movie set and I'll go with you again."

I wasn't sure I should follow the cat's advice, but what did I have to lose? Well, other than maybe going to jail or appearing crazy.

"How about after work today?" I asked.

"It sounds like a plan," Heather said.

She waved over her shoulder on the way out the door.

Chapter 16

*Charlotte's Handy-Dandy Tips
for Navigating the Afterlife*

*Talk into recorders and other electronic devices
because the living can hear you.*

I placed a few phone calls, lined up some appointments to see vintage clothing, and looked in the paper for a few estate sales. Sure enough, a few more ladies came in to buy dresses for the upcoming swing dance. After being busy with customers all day, when it came time to close, I wanted to go straight home and relax with a book. But I'd promised Heather that we would go to the film set. If I didn't go, I wouldn't be able to stop thinking about the message from Wind Song. Now every time I thought of the Fairtree Plantation, I had a vision of Nicole and the photos on Vera's wall.

I hoped Dylan called soon. What excuse would Vera give him for having the pictures of Nicole?

I supposed it wasn't illegal to be a fan and a photo collector, no matter how strange her display may be. No doubt she would want to know how he saw the photos. He would have to make up an excuse. Then again, he could just use the one I'd given him.

As I locked the door and stepped out onto the sidewalk, someone called my name. I spun around to see Ken Harrison waving at me as he headed down the sidewalk. I smiled and waved back. He wore a beige suit, a white shirt, and a blue tie. The colors looked good with his blond hair.

"Good afternoon," he said.

"How are you?" I asked.

"Things are okay. I'm glad that I spotted you," he said.

"Oh?" I asked.

Charlotte and Alice waited in the car for me. I knew they wouldn't stay there long because they would want to know what Ken had to say.

Ken motioned over his shoulder. "I noticed the café down the street. Would you like to get coffee?"

Charlotte and Alice would probably tell me to go with him and that the movie set could wait. But I wanted to speak with Jessica now. Wind Song hadn't spelled out that name for nothing.

"I'm sorry, I can't. I already have other plans."

Ken nodded, but the smile faded from his face.

Heather stepped out from her shop and was locking the door. When she turned around, she noticed Ken.

She mouthed, "What does he want?"

He saw that I was looking at something, so he glanced over his shoulder at her.

She smiled and threw up her hand in a wave. I was hoping she wouldn't tell him that we were going to the movie set.

He faced me again. "Some other time, then?"

I was off the hook. "Yes, I'd like that."

"Have a great day," he said with a smile.

"You too," I said.

Heather grinned at him, and he nodded.

Heather hurried over. "What was that all about?"

I knew I would have to be honest with her. "He asked if I wanted to get coffee."

"And you told him no?"

I turned toward the car. "We have to talk with Jessica. That's the most important thing right now."

Heather slipped into the passenger seat. "I suppose you're right. But I wonder what he wanted to talk about."

Charlotte threw her hands up. "Have you lost your cotton pickin' mind? Why didn't you go with him?"

"There will be time for that later." I shoved the key into the ignition.

When I glanced in the rearview mirror, Alice was shaking her head. "I hope there is a later. What if he never asks again?"

"That's a chance I'm willing to take." I turned down Magnolia Street and headed away from town.

Within a few minutes, we arrived at the plantation. I expected to see a security guard or someone to stop me this time, but I drove right into the parking lot and found a place up close to the path that led to the crew trailers.

I shoved the car into park and turned off the engine. Before I could unfasten my seat belt, Charlotte and Alice had gotten out of the car and were walking toward the set. Heather and I hurried toward them, but they didn't look as if they were going to wait on us or as if they even cared if we came along. Charlotte and Alice were on a mission.

"The ghosts left us behind," I said as we tried to catch up.

"I have a feeling they'll be back around soon enough," Heather said.

She was right about that. The last rays of sunshine turned to beautiful shades of deep navy blue and orange as Heather and I made the trip toward the trailers. A slight breeze stirred the magnolia leaves. A rabbit hopped from a nearby bush and dashed across the lush green lawn.

Heather jumped. "I guess I'm a little on edge. I thought it might be Vera Lemon leaping out at us."

The thought had briefly crossed my mind too. So far there was no sign of Vera, and I hadn't heard from Dylan about if he'd spoken with her. I was more than a little anxious to find out.

When we neared the trailers, I spotted Charlotte and Alice waiting for us up ahead. One person I didn't see, though, was the blond-haired security guard. Not that I was complaining, because I was glad that he wasn't there to question us. So far we hadn't seen anyone. I wondered if the crew had stopped filming and left the set. Alice waved when she saw me.

"Jessica's trailer is the silver one over there, right?" I asked.

"I think so. At least I hope so," Heather said.

I climbed up the steps of the trailer and knocked on the door. Silence filled the air and nothing sounded from inside.

"Maybe she's sleeping," Heather said.

I shrugged. "Maybe."

I knocked again, but still there was no sound. I was a little anxious that the assistant would yank the door open again.

"I don't think anyone is going to answer," Charlotte said.

Alice and Charlotte were standing next to Heather at the foot of the steps. What would I do now?

"You should try the door," Charlotte said.

That wasn't something that I wanted to do, but I didn't have many options—other than to leave once again without speaking with Jessica. Sending the ghosts in to look around wasn't a choice because I needed to see the trailer firsthand. They may miss something, and it was too important for that to happen. I didn't want to leave without at least giving it my best shot, so I reached out and grabbed the doorknob. My heart thumped faster as I turned the knob. The latch clicked, and then I knew that it was open. Was I really doing this? I would just poke my head in and call out to Jessica. There was no harm in that, right?

I opened the door just a crack and stuck my head in. So far no one was in sight. I saw a small white sofa and chair, a kitchenette area, and beyond that a closed door. Jessica's bed must have been in there.

"Hello, Jessica? Are you here?" I called out.

Still no one answered. Apparently once again I'd missed her. Another wasted trip. I looked back toward Heather, Charlotte, and Alice.

"She's not here."

Heather moved up a couple steps. "We should go in there."

I made a time-out signal with my hands. "What? We can't do that. What if someone catches us? We'll be arrested."

"Oh, go ahead. What is the worst that could happen?" Charlotte pushed.

"Well, they could be arrested," Alice said.

"Thank you, Alice," I said.

"No one is around." Heather gestured with a wave of her hand.

"That's true. Okay, we'll go in for just a second and have a little look."

I wasn't sure what we were looking for, but I was kind of curious nonetheless. I'd never been inside a movie star's trailer before.

I eased the door open and called out again, "Jessica, are you here?"

When she didn't answer, I stepped in and motioned for Heather to follow me. As we stood in the middle of the living room area, I said, "Now what?"

"What's behind that door?" Heather pointed.

"I don't know. I guess maybe a bed."

"We should take a look."

I glanced around again. "I guess we could take a little peek. We've already come this far. What's invading her privacy a little more, right?"

Heather chuckled. "Exactly."

We moved over to the closed door. When I glanced back, Charlotte and Alice were standing in the trailer too. Heather and I pushed forward toward the closed door. I grabbed the knob and turned. This door was unlocked too. Why had Jessica left all the doors unlocked?

We inched into the small space. It was really only enough room for one, so Heather and I were practically falling over each other. The only piece of furniture in the room was the bed. It was unmade with a pink blanket crumbled up in the middle of it.

Something else on the bed caught my attention right away—I was sure that all of the clothing that I'd given Nicole to wear on the movie set was there. How had Jessica gotten the items? Did Nicole give them to her before she died? Or had someone else given Jessica the pieces after Nicole had been murdered?

"Look at the things on the bed." I pointed.

"Yeah, she's kind of messy," Heather said.

"No, not that. These were all the items I'd provided for Nicole to wear."

"Well, her assistant did say that Jessica was supposed to take over Nicole's role."

"But these are all things that they weren't using anymore. Shiloh was supposed to have them returned to me."

"Hmm. That is odd. You should ask Shiloh about it."

That was exactly what I planned to do. Maybe the cat was onto something, after all. Maybe Jessica really did have something to do with this. After all, there were the text messages and now this. The thought sent a shiver down my spine.

It was time for us to get out of there. I decided to leave the items on the bed. I couldn't take them back yet. I would ask Shiloh about them first.

Heather and I hurried out of the trailer. Charlotte and Alice had already taken off and were waiting outside for us. I was just glad that we'd gotten out of there before getting caught. When I reached the bottom of the steps, I spotted Jessica across the way. She was headed toward the trailer. So far she hadn't seen us because she was too busy looking down at her cell phone.

"Here she comes," I said in a bit of a panic.

Heather had already started toward the car. She whipped around and looked in Jessica's direction. "Uh-oh. What do we do now?" she asked.

I could have run toward the Buick, but I really

wanted to talk with Jessica. I would just wait right here and act as if we'd just gotten here.

"Let's wait here for her," I said, motioning for Heather to come back.

"Are you going to ask her about the clothing?" Charlotte asked.

"That's my plan, yes."

Jessica still hadn't looked up from her phone. Then a man on a golf cart stopped her. They spoke, and then she hopped in the cart.

"Where is she going?" Heather asked.

"I don't know, but there goes my chance to talk with her again."

They drove down the path and never even looked over toward the trailer to notice us there. I could have yelled out at her, but that would have been a little too awkward.

"I think they're going to the parking lot," I said. "Come on, let's go."

Heather and I rushed toward the parking lot. Of course, Charlotte and Alice had left us once again.

"Too bad they couldn't have given us a ride," Heather said, huffing.

When we got to the edge of the parking lot, I spotted the cart. The man had dropped Jessica off at her car, a red Jaguar, and she was opening the door. She still hadn't noticed that anyone else was around. Heather and I raced toward my Buick as Jessica backed her car out of the spot.

The man on the golf cart looked our way when he drove by. He just waved. Apparently, it didn't bother him that we looked as if we were being chased by a bear. I guess he hadn't put two and two together that we were following Jessica. I cranked the engine. With the ghosts in the backseat and Heather in the front, I backed out and took off after Jessica's Jag. She turned onto the main road, and I pulled out right behind her.

"She's going to think you are a stalker," Charlotte said.

"I sure hope I'm good at stalking," I said.

Chapter 17

Don't forget to check the men's section.
You can find a number of cool items there,
like shirts, ties, or belts.

We followed Jessica through town, and she gave no indication she knew I was behind her. Most of the time, she was looking down at her phone. I had no idea how she hadn't wrecked yet.

"I wish she'd put that phone down and stop texting," Charlotte said.

"You and me both," I said.

"She's making me nervous," Alice said in a shaky voice.

"I think she's pulling into the hotel parking lot." Heather pointed.

I cut the wheel and made a right turn into the parking lot too. This was the same hotel where I'd met Shiloh the other day. Was she visiting Shiloh? We had to see what this visit was all about.

I whipped my Buick into a spot about three down from where Jessica parked. She jumped out of her car and strode toward the hotel's entrance. She was still looking at her phone. She would glance up every once in a while, I guess to keep from tripping.

"Why is she always in such a hurry?" Heather asked as she rushed beside me.

"I don't know. Doesn't she know that we don't do things fast around here? Nothing's going anywhere. That hotel will still be there in five minutes."

Jessica disappeared through the revolving doors. Heather and I were just a few steps behind her now. We pushed through the door and came into the lobby. The main desk was on the left, a large sitting area to the right.

"There she is," I said, pointing toward the lobby area.

Jessica stood with her back to us. Then she pressed the phone to her ear.

I stopped. "Looks like she's calling someone."

"Probably the person she's here to meet," Charlotte said.

Jessica had no sooner lowered the phone than Preston walked up to her. I rushed over to the potted dieffenbachia in the corner and motioned for Heather to follow me.

"I don't want them to see us," I whispered.

Heather squeezed in beside me, one of the leaves hitting her in the face.

"I don't think that's going to conceal both of you," Charlotte said.

"I don't have anywhere else to hide," I said.

"So don't hide. Let her know you are here. Go confront her." Alice motioned.

I scowled at her. "Have you lost your mind? I can't do that."

"So this is what it feels like to be paparazzi?" Heather said.

I chuckled. "I don't like the job."

I peeked out from behind one of the giant leaves.

"What are they doing now?" Heather asked.

"They're still talking."

"I still say you should march right up there and confront her," Alice said.

I wasn't listening to any of her advice.

"We can't stay like this for much longer because one of the employees will notice us. They may call the police," Heather said.

How many times recently had we worried the police may be called on us? I'd lost count. Jessica and Preston stood close to each other. She touched his arm several times, and they laughed. I wondered what was so funny. Probably some insider actor humor that we wouldn't understand.

"What is the woman behind the front desk doing? Is she watching us?" I asked.

Heather peeked to her left. "No, not right now. That's not to say she won't notice us at any moment and tell us to get out of here. I've never been kicked out of a hotel before."

"I've never been kicked out of anywhere before," I said.

"Well, I should hope not," Charlotte said.

Something like that would go against Charlotte's whole Southern upbringing. Of course, it would have made my mother fairly unhappy too. I didn't want to have to tell her I'd been kicked out of the Plaza. Leaves poked me in the face as I peeked out from the side of the plant again. That was when I saw Preston grab Jessica's hand.

"Oh, now they're holding hands," I said.

"What?" Heather inched her way up and pushed the leaves to each side. "I can't believe it," she said in disbelief.

"Next thing you know they'll kiss," Charlotte said.

She was probably right about that.

"We can't just wait around," I said.

"Oh, now they're walking away," Heather said.

I stuck my head out just in time to see Jessica and Preston strolling down the hallway hand in hand.

"Where are they going?" I asked.

"If you have to ask that, Cookie, then I can't help you," Charlotte said.

Preston certainly hadn't waited long before moving on with someone new. He had probably been seeing Jessica at the same time he'd been dating Nicole. And to think he had claimed to be engaged to Nicole. What a hound dog.

Heather and I stepped out from behind the plant.

"Well, I will have to talk to her later," I said.

"I guess we should leave," Heather said, sounding forlorn.

"At least you didn't get kicked out of the hotel," Alice said.

"Is the woman at the desk watching us?" I asked.

Heather leaned over. "No, I think we're clear to leave now."

My friend and I casually walked through the lobby. As we headed to the door, I spotted Shiloh, the film crew's costume manager.

"Look who it is," I said.

Heather looked back.

"And she's wearing that blue Dior gown that was Nicole's. Come on, we should talk to her. I want to ask about the other clothing that she was supposed to have returned by last week."

I turned on my heel and marched over to Shiloh. She was picking up a bottle of water that had been left for the guests on a table in the hallway.

"Maybe she was supposed to meet Jessica in the lobby," Charlotte said. "It looks as if she's waiting for someone."

When we neared Shiloh, I called out, "How are you, Shiloh?"

She whipped around, looked to Heather and then back to me again.

She forced a smile on her lips. "Oh, hello, Cookie. What are you doing here?"

"I thought I'd stop by and ask about the clothing again. Can you tell me when I'll be getting it back? Those are valuable pieces, you know."

Her smile disappeared. She took a drink from the water bottle while we waited. She took a few more sips before finally placing the lid back on the bottle.

Shiloh was acting strange, like she didn't want to answer. But since Heather and I were staring at her, there was little way she could get out of it. Too bad she didn't know that Charlotte and Alice were watching her too.

Putting the empty bottle into a nearby trash can, she looked at me and said, "Oh yes, the clothing from the movie set."

"Yes, that clothing. The reason you all hired me for the movie in the first place," I said.

She released a deep breath and then said, "To be perfectly honest with you, I can't find the items."

I stared at her in disbelief. "What do you mean?"

"Well, some of the garments were missing."

Yeah, I knew which items they were too. I'd seen them at Jessica's trailer. I wondered if I should tell her about that. No, then I would have to explain why I'd been there. I'd let it go for a while and see if Shiloh located the garments.

"This is bad," I said.

"I realize that and we will pay for any of the pieces that aren't returned."

I decided to press my advantage. "I couldn't help but notice your dress. Nicole bought it at my shop. I'm surprised to see you wearing it."

Her eyes widened. "This is my dress," she said.

"Oh, Nicole gave it to you?" I asked.

She scowled. "No, I brought this dress from home. It is mine."

"That is a rare dress. Where did you find it?"

She glared at me. "I don't remember. I've had it for a very long time."

I wasn't buying that story. I knew my clothing, and that dress had come from my shop.

She grabbed another bottle of water and walked past us. "I'll bring the clothing by, or money, soon."

Shiloh marched down the hallway.

"She's lying about the dress?" Alice asked.

"Yes, a big fat lie," I said.

Shiloh stepped onto the elevator, the doors closing on her scowling face.

"That didn't go well," Heather said.

"No, it didn't. What do we do now?" I asked.

"How about you go find Ken and take him up on his offer?" Charlotte said.

"Now that is the best idea I've heard all day," Alice said.

I headed out across the lobby toward the exit. "You know, I hate to say this, but the ghosts might be right. Maybe I do need to have coffee with Ken."

"I have to agree," Heather said.

We climbed into the Buick and headed back to my shop. After dropping Heather off, I picked up Wind Song and headed for home. That night, I picked up the phone several times thinking that I would call Ken, but I never dialed. I also almost called Dylan's number, but chickened out. That didn't make Charlotte and Alice happy, but I couldn't please the ghosts all the time.

I climbed into bed while Charlotte and Alice discussed the (to them) obvious reasons why I should have called both men. I put in my earplugs and covered my head with the pillow, begging sleep to spare me from their inane chatter.

Chapter 18

Charlotte's Handy-Dandy Tips
for Navigating the Afterlife

For fun entertainment—because let's face it,
being a ghost can get boring—
hide items from the living.
It's a real hoot to watch them search for their stuff.

The next morning, I was at the shop early because I had paperwork that I had neglected recently. Although I had a part-time accountant, I tried to keep track of my cash flow myself—both to save money and to feel I was running my business efficiently. I'd worn a white-and-yellow floral Parnes Feinstein dress with a yellow rose in my hair. My white sandals completed the casual summer look.

The ghosts were bored while I was busy with work. They still wanted to discuss the case. But frankly, I was getting nowhere with it and needed a break. It made me feel better to take my mind off the investigation and focus on invoices and bank statements. When I finished the paperwork, I needed to bring some clothing out from the back and place the items on hangers.

The items had just been cleaned and were ready for the floor. Some of them might even end up in the front window on a mannequin. The ghosts followed me to the back storage room. I had racks of clothing that were being processed or mended and a couple of chairs for break time. A small desk in the far corner was covered with boxes of vintage shoes that needed polishing or repairs. I sifted through the clothing and found the items that I needed—a wonderful collection of pleated swimsuits that would have looked good on Esther Williams. I could just picture my mannequins wearing them in the display window, surrounded by colorful beach balls and parasols.

"Are you going to call Ken and Dylan today?" Alice asked.

"Maybe." I concentrated on sorting through the clothing.

"That's not the answer we were looking for," Charlotte said.

I didn't respond. From the front, the doorbell jingled.

"If you'll excuse me, ladies, I need to wait on a customer."

Charlotte stepped in front of me. "Not until you agree to call them."

Alice stood beside her, looking equally determined.

My mouth dropped. "You two are seriously holding me hostage until I agree to call them?"

"This is for your own good," Alice said.

I rolled my eyes. "Yeah, right." I pushed toward the women, and my hands went right through them.

"Oh, don't do that," Charlotte said when I walked through their arms.

"Then don't stand in my way."

I reached the door and twisted the knob, but nothing happened.

"The door won't open," I said. "What did you all do to it?"

Charlotte placed her hands on her hips. "I am offended that you would think I would do such a thing."

"Well, forgive me, but you just tried to keep me back here until I agreed to do what you want me to do."

"I am a lady and would never do something like that to you," she said.

"Then why is it stuck?" I asked.

Alice and Charlotte shrugged.

"Maybe it's just the humidity," Alice said.

I supposed it was possible.

"Just push on it harder," Charlotte said.

I placed my hand on the knob and my shoulder against the door. I twisted and gave it a good shove. Nothing happened. I was starting to panic. What if I was stuck in here?

I shoved again, but I couldn't get the door open. I wiped my forehead and released a deep breath. I had to calm down. I didn't like being in small places.

"Don't panic, Cookie, the door will open. Everything will be just fine," Alice said.

The bell over the front door jingled again. I wasn't sure if the customer had left or if another customer had come in, but I couldn't leave the store unattended for long. Even in Sugar Creek, shoplifting could happen, and my shop was full of valuable items. I would have to get out of there.

I tried to calm down and pushed the door again, but I had the same outcome. I'd never had any problems with this door before. After this, I would never shut it again.

"Hello?" I called out. "I'm back here. I can't get the door open."

No one answered. I wasn't sure if that was because they couldn't hear me or were afraid to answer. Either way, no one answered or came to help me.

"Okay." I released a deep breath. "Can you all see who is out there?"

Charlotte and Alice answered in unison, "Of course."

They floated through the door. Now if I could just figure out a way that they could get the door unstuck for me. I tapped my foot against the floor and fidgeted while I waited for them to return. What were they doing? What were they waiting for? I was freaking out wondering what was happening on the other side of that door.

"Hello?" I called out. "What are you gals doing? Did you forget about me?"

Finally, Charlotte and Alice popped back in. I couldn't read the looks on their faces.

"Well, what is going on? Is there a customer out there?"

Charlotte shook her head. "No one is out there."

"Great. I missed a customer. How unprofessional is that?"

"That's not the worst of the problems," Charlotte said.

"Okay, now you're scaring me. What happened?"

"There's a chair against the door. It's under the knob. That's why you can't get out."

The color probably drained from my face. Who would have done that? Why had they locked me in this room? Luckily, I remembered that I had my cell phone in my pocket. I pulled it out and dialed Heather. There was no telling how long I would have had to stay in there if I hadn't had the phone. I prayed that she would pick up because I didn't want to call 911

After I explained the bizarre situation to Heather, she said she would be right over. I hoped that the person who did this wasn't still in the store. What if Heather ran into the intruder? Maybe I should have called the police. After all, someone had done this on purpose. It wasn't an accident. Someone wanted me to stay in that room. What would Dylan say when I told him about this? After a couple minutes, the bell rang again. I hoped it was Heather this time.

"Cookie, I'm here," she called out.

"Thank goodness," I said.

The sound of the chair moving away from the door gave me some relief. Heather yanked on the door.

"Are you okay?" she grabbed my arm and pulled me out of the room.

"I'm fine."

Heather looked around the shop. "Who do you think did this?"

I blew the hair out of my eyes. "I honestly don't know. But I think someone was trying to give me a message. And that message has been received loud and clear."

Heather scooted the chair away from the door. "What were you doing when it happened?"

"I was in there getting a few pieces of clothing. The ghosts were nagging me about calling Ken and Dylan. I really thought I'd left the door open."

Heather frowned. "That's a scary thought."

"Yes, it is."

Wind Song was standing beside me, meowing. Heather and I exchanged a look.

"Do you think she saw who did it?" Heather asked.

"Would she be able to tell us if she did?" I asked.

"You should get the Ouija board back out and see," Alice said.

"We need to use the Ouija board," Heather said.

Charlotte chimed in, "I agree."

It was a good thing I agreed, because I would have been outnumbered. Heather and I left the back of the store and went to the counter. I was still trying to figure out who would have locked me in and why.

When I reached the counter, I pulled up a stool. I needed to sit down and recover from my panic.

"What are these cards doing here?" Heather asked, pointing to tarot cards on top of the counter.

Three cards sat on top of the counter. I'd never seen them before.

"They're not yours?" I asked.

She shook her head. "No, I didn't have them."

"The cards weren't there when I went to the back."

Heather stepped closer and picked up each card, examining them.

"They're not the cards that Wind Song has been using. And they're not the cards that I use."

"Who else would have tarot cards around here?" Alice asked.

I tucked a strand of hair behind my ear. "I honestly don't know. There's no one else who uses the tarot cards that I know."

"What about Heather? Does she know who uses the cards?" Charlotte asked.

"Charlotte wants to know if anyone else in town uses the tarot cards," I translated.

"Several people, but they wouldn't leave them here. These cards look relatively new, as if they hadn't been purchased long ago."

"This is certainly strange." Alice paced across the space in front of the counter.

"So what do the cards mean?" I asked, gesturing toward them.

Heather held each card up, one at a time.

"This card is the justice card. Its meaning is for justice of the universe, not really justice in law or revenge. This card is the fool. Its meaning is for moving forward. And this card is the death card. Its meaning is for transformation, not really death."

"That combination of cards is definitely trying to send you a message," Charlotte said.

"Did they leave these cards on purpose?" I asked. "Meaning the message was that I'm a fool and they will get revenge with death?"

"Good thinking," Alice said.

Heather frowned. "I think so, yes. But this person couldn't know anything about the tarot cards because he or she would know that these are not the literal meanings."

"I don't think that matters to them. They just wanted to threaten me."

"Well, it worked" Heather placed the cards back on the counter. "We need to use the Ouija board. I'll be right back."

As Heather hurried out to retrieve the board, I studied the cards.

"Try not to worry, sugar. I'm sure that everything will be fine," Charlotte said.

Alice stepped close. "I'm sorry that I got you involved in this."

I shook my head. "Don't worry, Alice, you were just trying to help Nicole."

The bell sounded above the door, and I jerked up to look. I was on edge, thinking that the intruder might return. But it was Heather with the board under her arm. Maybe I needed to rethink my policy on not having a Ouija board of my own. It looked as if I was going to need one.

Heather placed the board down on the counter

once again. I set the planchette down in the middle, and we all looked toward the cat. Wind Song was still standing guard by the back door.

"It's okay, sweetie, you can come up here now," I said.

She licked her paws and stared at us. If she came up, it would be on her own terms.

"Offer her a treat," Charlotte said.

Before I had a chance to retrieve the bag of treats from under the counter, Wind Song strolled toward us. Just the mention of treats had worked. The cat hopped up on the counter.

"Maybe she doesn't want to use it," I said.

Heather shrugged. "I guess we're about to find out."

"Or maybe she saw nothing," Alice added. "Cats can sleep through anything."

I wished the ghost gals had seen who had been in the store. If only they'd taken a peek out there a little sooner. Wind Song swayed her tail and placed her paw on the planchette.

"I'd say she wants to use it," Heather said.

The cat pushed the planchette around the board. All eyes were focused on the board. The first letter was *H*. Wind Song pushed to the second letter, which was *U*. Then she moved it to the *N*.

"*Hun?*" Heather said.

"She's not finished," I said.

Wind Song moved to the *G* and then to the *R*.

"I think I see where this is going," I said.

The cat just spelled out that she was hungry.

Charlotte and Alice laughed. "Okay, Wind Song. Message received"

Wind Song pushed the planchette again.

"Do you want to tell me what kind of food now?" I asked.

Alice snickered. Wind Song pushed the planchette to another letter. This time it was the *J*. Heather and I exchanged a quick glance. Then Wind Song moved it to the *E*. Next was *S* followed by another *S*. The cat was going to spell the name *Jessica* again.

"Is that who was in here and placed the chair under the door?" I asked.

Wind Song licked her paws and then meowed. I retrieved her food dish from under the counter.

"I don't think we'll get another answer from her," I said.

Heather leaned against the counter. "Probably not."

Was Wind Song just stuck on the same name, though? Maybe it had nothing to do with what had just happened. I couldn't know for sure. I placed the dish on the counter and put some gourmet tuna in it. She ate, and I rubbed her head.

"Thanks for the message, Wind Song," I said.

She hadn't given me an answer, but it was better than nothing.

"Do you think it was Jessica?" Heather asked.

"It's possible. Why else would Wind Song give us her name?"

When Wind Song finished the food, she licked her paws and jumped from the counter. She strolled to the front of the store and curled up in her favorite spot in the sun. At least she wasn't afraid to go back to the front of the store now. She had seemed a little spooked earlier. She probably hadn't liked that someone had been in the store while I was locked in the back.

"This was the second time Wind Song gave us Jessica's name," Heather said.

"Yeah, she may only know that one name," I said.

"Or the cat knows exactly who did it and just told us."

I tapped my fingers against the counter.

Heather picked up the board. "I'm putting the board away this time. Every time we use this thing, Dylan stops in. I don't want him to catch us."

"You should just tell him about the board and the tarot cards," Alice said.

I shook my head. "No way. I definitely can't tell him that the cat uses them and gives me messages."

"That is a bit far-fetched," Heather said.

"I wouldn't know where to begin to explain how the cat communicates with us."

"So show him. Let the cat use the board and the cards when he's here," Alice said.

"She probably wouldn't do it in front of him," I said.

"You're probably right. She's too shy," Heather said.

"Well, apart from that, I must tell Dylan about the cards we found and the chair under the doorknob."

Heather agreed. "It's best that you do. If someone is messing with you, then he needs to know."

"It is a little embarrassing to admit that I was locked in the back room."

Plus, I knew that by keeping anything I'd discovered to myself would give me a chance to solve the crime first. Why didn't I just leave this to the professionals?

"You had no control over that," Charlotte said.

"Yes, Cookie, there's nothing you could have done to stop it," Alice said.

They were right. I pulled out my phone and dialed Dylan's number.

"At least she has his number memorized," Charlotte said.

I frowned, but didn't respond. When he picked up, I had the sudden urge to hang up. I wondered if I really needed to bother him with this tiny detail. But then I realized it wasn't a tiny detail. It was important that he know this.

"Dylan, hi, it's Cookie."

"So cute that they're on a first-name basis," Charlotte said.

I waved my hand to quiet Charlotte. Alice chuckled. I was glad that they thought this was so entertaining. After I told him what had happened, he said he would be over right away.

"He's on his way," I said when I hung up the phone.

"You did the right thing," Heather said.

"I just hope we find who did this. The person needs to be brought to justice," I said.

"We won't stop until we do," Alice said.

Chapter 19

*You can mix the old with the new.
Don't be afraid to pair a fifties skirt
with a top you just bought at the mall.*

Within minutes, Detective Dylan Valentine walked through the door. He wore dark blue slacks and one of the shirts that he'd bought from my store—the blue one that matched his eyes. I couldn't help but smile when I saw him.

When he reached the counter, he said, "Hi, Cookie. Hello, Heather. Is everyone okay?"

I nodded. "We're fine now."

He glanced down and noticed the tarot cards. "You say someone locked you in the back room? How did that happen?"

I explained the sequence of events.

"How do you know someone locked you in?" he asked. "Maybe the door was just stuck."

"I thought so at first, but then I called Heather.

She came over and discovered the chair was pushed under the knob."

I had to leave out the part about the ghosts peeking out there and spotting the chair first.

He looked at Heather. "So the chair was under the knob?" His eyebrows pinched together in a frown.

Heather's eyes were solemn. "Yes, that's exactly what happened."

"You said something about receiving a threatening message? What was that?" he asked.

This was the part I had been dreading telling him about.

I pointed out the cards. "Well, we found these tarot cards on the counter. They're not mine and they're not Heather's. We have no idea where they came from."

He picked up the cards and studied them. "What do they mean?"

Heather stepped closer. "That is the fool card. That one is the justice card and that one is the death card."

"What does all this mean?" he asked. "How is it threatening?"

"Well, I figured out that it means I am the fool who will get revenge, meaning death," I said.

"Yeah, but the person obviously doesn't know how to read the cards," Heather said.

"How so?" Dylan asked.

"Because the cards are Justice, Fool, and Death, but those aren't the true meanings of the cards.

So the person who left them wouldn't have experience in reading cards as far as I can tell," Heather said.

Dylan ran his hand through his hair. "I see. That makes sense. And you didn't see anyone near the counter?"

I shook my head. "No, not at all."

Heather tapped her forehead as a realization struck. "You know, I sold cards like that about a month ago."

Dylan looked over at her. "Really?"

"I carry a few different styles. I usually sell about four sets a month. Not too many, but they are fairly popular."

"Do you have any idea who you would have sold a set like this to?" Dylan asked.

I had my fingers crossed that Heather would remember. Alice and Charlotte moved closer.

"I really can't recall," she said.

Oh well, at least we had tried.

"Whoever I sold them to wouldn't have been anyone who was connected to Nicole, though. I would remember anyone from the movie coming into the store." Heather sounded confident of her words.

Dylan wrote something on a pad he'd pulled from his pocket. I thought about leaning closer, but figured that wouldn't be the best idea. After he finished writing, he folded the tablet and stuffed it back into his shirt pocket. "Can you look up info of who made the cards? Maybe the person bought them somewhere other than your store."

She nodded. "Sure, I can do that."

It hadn't occurred to me that the person could have bought the cards from somewhere other than Heather's shop. I just assumed that any occult items would have been purchased from her place. I hoped we'd be able to track down the source soon.

"Okay, I have a mission." Heather gave a mock salute and headed for the door.

"Good luck," I said and waved.

"I'm glad you called and told me about this," Dylan said.

"Better safe than sorry." It sent a shiver down my spine to think the killer had been in my shop. And that the person had possibly threatened me.

I sat on the stool again. "I wanted to ask you about Vera Lemon. Did you talk to her and find out why she had all the photos of Nicole on her wall?"

Dylan seemed to choose his words carefully. "Yes, I did speak with her. Ms. Lemon explained that she was a fan of Nicole's. She had the photos because she just really liked her."

"That's a whole lot of like," I said.

He grinned. "Yes, it is."

"Did she have anything else to say about it?"

"Not really. And there's not much we can do without any other evidence to go on," he said.

"Yes, that's understandable."

Charlotte rested on the settee. "Vera had more

photos on that wall than a preteen collecting posters from a *Tiger Beat* magazine."

I bit back a smile.

"Sorry it didn't turn up more clues," Dylan was saying.

I waved off his comment. "You have a lot to take care of. I just wish I could help more."

"You helped a bunch by telling me about the photos. It was odd, to say the least, but we can't prove anything."

I picked at a blouse from the counter. "Sure. It would be hard to prove anything from just a collection of photos."

"I'm glad that you called me today and shared this with me." His voice softened and made the Southern drawl even sexier.

"I thought it was something you should know."

"Are you going to be okay?" Dylan searched my eyes.

I picked at the hem of my shirt. "I'll be fine. It was just a little unsettling."

"Yes, I can see where that would be the case."

There was a silence, and then I said, "I like your shirt."

A smile twisted at the corners of his mouth. "I think it's my new favorite shirt."

It made my heart happy that he enjoyed the vintage clothing. I'd hoped he hadn't bought the items just to have a reason to ask me questions about the case. Although I guess he really wouldn't need an excuse.

Just then Heather burst back through the door. "I remember who I sold the cards to," she said.

I jumped up from the stool. "That's great news."

"Who is it?" Dylan asked.

"Her name is Faith Lauren. She does readings and stuff."

"And you definitely remember selling the cards to her?" Dylan asked.

Heather was practically hopping with excitement. "Yes, I remember it clearly now. It just popped back into my head."

"Do you know anything else about her?" Dylan asked.

"Yes, I know her a little. As a matter of fact, I know where she is right now."

We all stared at Heather.

"Where is she?" I asked, not able to stand the suspense.

"She's at the Plaza Hotel. There's a paranormal conference there this weekend. It's just a small get-together, but there are a few people doing readings. Faith has a table set up there this weekend to do readings. I really don't think she would have left her cards here though."

That was what I had been wondering.

Dylan asked, "Do you want to visit this person?"

I was a little shocked that he had asked me.

"Sure," I said, looking at Heather.

"Don't worry. I'll watch the shop for you."

I just hoped the intruder didn't come back in while Heather was there.

"Don't go into the back room," I warned.

"You can count on that." Heather assured me.

"Oh, good, a road trip," Charlotte said.

Oh no. I wished I could tell her she couldn't come. But I couldn't, and I knew the ghosts wouldn't listen either. As long as they were quiet, I guess it wouldn't be so bad.

"Are you ready?" Dylan asked.

I got my purse. "Yes, let's go."

Dylan and I walked outside to his police car. His unmarked car was gray, with lights in the back windows. Charlotte and Alice were right there. By the time I'd gotten into the passenger seat, they were settled in behind us. At least Dylan hadn't made me ride in the prisoner's seat. I never wanted to be back there.

We barely pulled away from the curb when my cell phone rang.

"I'm sorry, but I was mistaken," I heard Heather say. "The conference was last weekend."

"What? Oh no," I said.

Dylan glanced over at me. "What's wrong?"

"Don't worry," she said. "I know her address. You can just go to her house."

"Thank goodness."

Dylan glanced at me again. "At least it was followed with good news."

"You're keeping us in suspense back here," Charlotte said.

I hung up with Heather. "The conference was last weekend, but Heather had Faith's address."

"Just tell me where to go and I'll point the car in that direction," Dylan said.

Chapter 20

We drove across town and pulled into a sub-division called Crystal Springs Estates. Dylan followed the directions Heather had given me and pulled right up to Faith Lauren's house. It was a white two story with black shutters. A lot of the houses looked alike on the street. The styles varied only slightly.

We walked up the driveway and then the stone path to the glossy black front door. A pot of red geraniums sat on the left and a pair of tennis shoes on the right. Dylan rang the doorbell, and after a few seconds a woman opened the door. Faith wore a white blouse with white shorts. She was barefoot, and her toenails were painted a bright red to match her fingertips.

"May I help you?" She looked from me to him.

Dylan pulled out his badge. "Detective Dylan Valentine. Sugar Creek Police. We wondered if we could ask you a few questions?"

Her eyes widened. She had short blond hair and big blue eyes rimmed with blue eyeliner. She hadn't asked us inside, not that I expected her to. She didn't even open the door all the way. Understandably, she looked suspicious of us.

"We were told you purchased a set of tarot cards from the Magic Marketplace recently."

She frowned. "That is an odd question."

"But you did purchase the cards?" Dylan pushed.

She said, "Yes, I did purchase a set from the store."

"And you use the cards on a regular basis?"

She looked at me again and then back to Dylan. "Yes, I do readings quite often."

Dylan nodded. "I see. Did you use the cards today?"

"Is this some kind of joke?" she asked.

Dylan looked right at her and said, "I can assure you that this is no joke. So you used the cards today?" he asked again.

Dylan had control of the questioning and wasn't about to give up on getting his answers.

"Actually, no, I didn't use the cards today. Because I don't know where the cards are."

Wow, I hadn't expected that answer.

"What do you mean?" Dylan asked.

"Last week I was at the Plaza doing some readings and halfway through the day someone took the cards. I had to stop because I didn't have another set."

"Do you know who took the cards?" Dylan pressed for more answers.

She shifted her weight from one foot to the other. "I have no idea, but I wish I knew. I wasn't happy that someone had stolen them. I thought maybe it was another psychic who didn't want the competition from me. But there were a lot of people around that day, so who knows? I guess it could have been anyone. And I'd just purchased the cards too. They were like new."

I remembered Heather saying that the cards were purchased recently. This had to be the same cards, right? It was too bad Faith didn't know who had taken the cards. Was she being honest?

She would have no reason to come into my shop and leave her cards though. We didn't even know each other.

"Is there anything else that you remember from that day?" Dylan asked.

Faith didn't hesitate. "Oh, there was one thing that was a little odd. That woman working on the movie set was there."

My eyes widened. Ah-ha. A connection to the film crew.

"Which woman was that?" Dylan asked.

"I don't remember her name."

I remembered that Shiloh had been staying at

the hotel. Then again, I'd seen Jessica there too when she'd met Preston.

"Did she have blond hair and blue eyes?" I asked.

Faith shrugged. "Yes, I think so."

"What about a small tattoo of a red rose on the back of her wrist?" I asked.

Faith looked at me in surprise. "Yes, I remember that."

"Thank you for the information," Dylan said.

"Did you come here to find my tarot cards?" Faith asked.

She looked completely confused.

"If we find the cards we'll make sure you get them back," he said.

I smiled at the woman, but she just looked at me blankly. I wished I had time to explain to her what was going on. Dylan and I hurried to his car. Faith watched us as we jumped in.

"Well, this just has a lot of twists and turns," Charlotte said.

"I'll say," Alice chimed in. "It's a good thing you have the handsome detective's help."

I knew they wouldn't be quiet in the backseat.

I fastened my seat belt and said, "Shiloh has a rose tattoo on the back of her wrist."

He smiled at me. "Good job. You have an eye for detail."

"It comes from being in the world of fashion." I smiled.

Dylan didn't speed to the hotel, but he drove as fast as the speed limit would allow. Within a few minutes, we were pulling into the parking lot. As soon as he shoved the car into park, I opened the door and rushed out.

"You are in a hurry," he said as he met me at the front of the car.

"I guess I'm a little anxious for answers."

Dylan and I headed for the revolving entrance door, with Charlotte and Alice in tow. The ghosts came with us through the doors. I would have just floated in if I were them. Dylan stepped up to the desk. I waited over at the side for him to speak with the manager, a dapper fortyish man with a pencil-thin mustache. I could still hear their conversation though. He'd asked for footage of any surveillance video during the conference at the hotel.

After a couple of minutes, he stepped over to where I stood. "They're going to get the footage for us to look at."

"That's great," I said.

"You've been a lot of help with this investigation," he said.

I smiled. "I just wanted to help."

He searched my eyes. "Why is that?"

I couldn't tell him that a ghost had made me do it. But to be honest, I wanted to see the killer in jail. I didn't want this kind of crime in my hometown. I was trying to come up with a quick and logical response when the manager motioned for us that the video was ready.

"I hope we'll see something there," Alice said as she followed us back to the manager's office.

"We have to ask Shiloh what she is doing," Charlotte said.

We filed into the small office and gathered around the small screen.

"This is the conference. Is there a time period you are looking for?" The manager asked in a smooth baritone.

Hmm. I hadn't thought of that. The conference had been several hours, and we couldn't watch all of them.

Dylan answered, "I'm not sure."

"Look, there's Faith Lauren." I pointed.

We watched the screen. The manager sped up the action.

"Wait," Dylan called out. "Stop the video."

Shiloh was sitting at the table getting a reading from Faith. When the reading was over, Shiloh stood and Faith turned away from the table. That was when Shiloh grabbed the cards and left the room.

"Wow, she took the cards."

"Thank you," Dylan said. "That's all that we needed. Can I get a copy of that?"

The manager nodded. "Of course."

When we stepped out of the office, I asked, "What do we do now?"

"We should talk with Shiloh."

"I know which room she's in."

He looked over at me.

"I had to see her about the costumes," I said.

He winked. "Right."

We headed through the lobby and to the elevators.

I looked back at the lobby and saw the plant where Heather and I had hidden. That seemed like ages ago. I wondered about that meeting between Preston and Jessica. Were they really seeing each other? Or was something else going on between them?

"She's in room 408," I said.

Dylan and I stepped onto the elevator, and he pushed the button for the fourth floor. I saw Charlotte's and Alice's reflections in the mirror. They were standing behind us.

"She may not want to admit to taking the cards," he said.

"I'd say it's a safe bet that she won't admit to it," Charlotte said.

"Why in the world would she want to take them? She could have just bought a set for herself," Alice said.

That was true, and I had no explanation for her irrational behavior. But then she had Nicole's dress too. And she hadn't admitted to taking it, even though I knew it was Nicole's. Maybe Shiloh had a problem with taking things that didn't belong to her.

We stepped off the elevator into the hall, then turned to the right in the direction of room 408. After a few seconds, we'd arrived in front of the door.

Dylan knocked.

"Who is it?" a voice called out. "I didn't order anything and I don't need towels."

Dylan knocked again, but still didn't say anything.

Bangs and a couple thuds sounded from behind the door. The lock clicked, and then Shiloh opened the door. Her eyes widened when she saw us. She knew me, and I knew she'd talked to Dylan before. She probably wondered why we were here together.

She leaned against the door and smiled. "What can I do for you all?"

She'd picked up a Southern accent since she'd arrived in Sugar Creek. I was curious if she had the clothing in the room or if she'd hidden it. Maybe she had the cards right out in the open too. She had to know why we were there.

"Good afternoon, Shiloh. Sorry for bothering you, but we had just a few questions."

She looked from Dylan to me. "Sure, is this about the murder? Because I already gave all the information I know."

"This isn't about that."

Technically, it was about the murder, but she didn't need to know that. I wondered if she'd be truthful when she found out we had evidence that she'd taken the cards. Her stance stiffened. She was acting nervous.

"This is about missing tarot cards."

Her face turned red, but she tried to keep her composure.

"Tarots cards? I don't know . . ."

She acted as if she was completely shocked by the question. Maybe she had aspirations of being an actress, but she shouldn't quit her day job.

"We have video of you taking the cards," Dylan said, not wasting time for her lies.

She stared, speechless.

"We spoke with Faith Lauren. She said she gave you a reading and then the cards were stolen. When we checked the hotel's footage, we saw you take them, put them in your purse, and walk out of the room."

"She called the police because her tarot cards were taken? And you all actually investigated this?" She stared at us.

I had to admit it was funny to see her stunned face.

Shiloh sighed. "Okay, I took the cards. It's not a felony, for heaven's sake. I can't believe she is making such a big deal out of it. It's not like she can't replace the cards. Plus, I doubt they cost that much anyway."

If they didn't cost much and Faith could easily replace them, then why did Shiloh take them?

"So are you going to arrest me?" she asked.

"No," Dylan said. "It would be up to Faith to press charges."

"Then why are you here? Just to harass me?" She glared at me.

"Like I said, we have some questions to ask," Dylan said.

"Other than asking about the cards?" She moved as if she wanted to shut the door on us, but I doubted Dylan would let that happen. "Look, I already told you everything I know about the murder.

I can't help you anymore. So I'm sorry about the cards. It was a bad decision."

She could say that again. But had she been the intruder who left the cards at my shop?

"Why did you take the cards?" Dylan asked.

Shiloh looked down at her bare feet. How long could she stall? Dylan stepped closer to the door, and her eyes widened.

"Okay, I took the cards because I didn't like the reading she gave me, okay? That's the reason."

"What did she tell you?" I asked.

"I asked her about someone and she said it wouldn't work out with that person."

That was hardly a reason to steal the woman's cards.

"So just because you didn't like her reading, you stole from her?" I asked.

"That's it. That's the only reason. Are you finished with the questions now?" She glanced over her shoulder.

"Actually, I'm not finished with the questions." Dylan looked over her shoulder. "Is there something you are keeping from me? Is there something in your room that you don't want me to see?"

She shifted to the left, trying to block his view. "Of course there's nothing I'm hiding."

Her words said one thing, but her body language said another.

She glared. "I just have a lot of work to do, that's all. And I'm really behind schedule."

"That's a shame. Now where are the cards?" Dylan asked, once again looking over her shoulder.

She scowled. "I don't have them. Sure, I took the cards, but I don't have them now." She gestured. "You can come in and look if you'd like."

Would she have invited us in if she had something to hide? Or was she calling our bluff? Anticipating that we wouldn't take her up on that offer?

"If you don't have the cards, then where are they now?" Dylan asked.

She'd probably say that she had dumped them in the trash. She was playing innocent, but it wouldn't work.

Shiloh said, "I gave the cards to Jessica. She seemed interested in them so I let her have them."

Why would Jessica want the cards? Had Jessica been the one to leave them in my shop?

"When did you give them to her?" Dylan asked.

"It was just yesterday. Why is there such a big deal about the cards? Were they special?" she asked.

"You could say that, yes." Dylan's voice was calm and professional.

I guess that meant that Dylan wasn't going to tell Shiloh about cards being left at my store. I supposed she didn't need to know that detail.

"Okay. Well, like I said, I am sorry that I took the cards. It won't happen again, I can promise you that. If I see Jessica I can tell her to give them back if that will help."

"No, that won't be necessary. In fact, I'd rather that you not mention this to her," Dylan said.

"Yeah, okay." Shiloh grasped the doorknob as if she couldn't wait for us to leave.

"Thank you for talking to us, Shiloh. I'll be in touch."

She scowled. "Sure, you're welcome."

I waved as we walked away. She returned my gesture with a frown.

As we neared the elevator, I said, "So we need to talk to Jessica, right? She had to be the one who left the cards. She can't claim that she gave the cards away. Do you think Shiloh was being honest?"

I was just full of questions. Dylan pressed the DOWN button.

"Yeah, I think she's being truthful. And you're right, the next stop is to ask Jessica about it."

Now would have been a good time for me to tell Dylan about the text messages. For some reason, I was silent.

The elevator door opened, and we stepped on.

"Maybe you shouldn't be there when I talk with Jessica."

I frowned. "Why do you think so?"

"Well, if she did leave the cards at your shop, she might not confess with you there."

That made sense. I really wanted to hear her explanation though. I wanted to see her face when we told her that we knew about the cards. She probably figured I would never find out that it was her. Okay, I didn't know for sure, but I had a feeling.

Dylan peeked at his gold watch. "I have an appointment now anyway. I'll go by later this afternoon and talk with her, then I'll come by your shop if you'll be there."

"Sure. I'll be there."

Maybe I'd be there when he arrived. Dylan may not want me to talk with Jessica with him, but I'd go to her trailer without him. Maybe I'd even beat him there. I hated to mess up his case, but he wasn't moving fast enough for me. I couldn't wait on him. I needed to act quickly. He didn't even need to know.

We got back in Dylan's police car and headed for my shop. It was a short drive, and we spent the time talking about the case. He didn't share any specifics with me that I didn't already know. I kind of felt guilty about going behind his back, but not enough to stop me from doing it. Dylan pulled up to the curb, and I jumped out. When I stepped around the car, he walked with me to the front door of the shop.

He flashed his dazzling smile at me. "I'll talk to you soon."

Butterflies did a brief fox-trot in my stomach. "See you later, gator."

Chapter 21

Cookie's Savvy Vintage Fashion Shopping Tips

Research the cost of items.
Know your budget and what you're willing
to pay for your favorite piece.

When I walked through the door, Heather tossed aside her crossword puzzle and jumped up. "What happened? I've been dying to find out."

"Please don't use that word," Alice said.

"We think Jessica has the cards," I told her.

Heather's mouth dropped open. "You're kidding. How did that happen?"

"Well, the cards were stolen from Faith and Shiloh is the one who took them."

"Shut up," Heather said. "Then how did Jessica get them?"

I filled Heather in on all that had happened.

"You're freaking Heather out with all the details," Charlotte said.

"I just can't believe it." Heather plopped down on the stool behind her.

I dropped onto the settee. "It's crazy."

"So what are you going to do now?"

"Dylan said he would talk with her later today after an appointment."

She smiled. "But you don't want to wait that long, right?"

"Exactly."

"I suppose you could close early today."

"And you too?" I asked.

She got up. "Of course."

"I don't know if I have a great feeling about this," Alice said.

Now she was worried? She was the one who wanted me to solve this crime. Now that I was making progress, I couldn't back out.

Heather and I wrapped up our work for the day and got into my Buick. Charlotte was pretty excited about the trip, but Alice was fidgeting in the backseat.

"Everything will be fine, Alice, don't worry. We'll track down Jessica and ask her about the cards." I steered onto the road.

After all, I had Heather with me, and it would be two against one. She couldn't do something to both of us, right? At least I hoped not. I pulled away from the curb and pointed the car toward the plantation.

The energy in the Buick was pretty charged. We were all anxious about what might happen. I was still trying to wrap my mind around the idea that

Jessica could have locked me in the back room. After all, what had I done to her?

"This is by far one of the most exciting things I've done," Alice said. "And I don't mean exciting in a good way. I mean, exciting as in if I were alive I would lose my cookies in the backseat."

"Good to know, Alice," I said.

We once again reached the plantation, and I pulled into the parking lot and found a space at the front. How many more times would we be able to sneak onto the set before I got caught? I hoped today wasn't the day that they tossed us out on our bottoms.

I shifted the car into park and cut the engine. "Are we ready, ladies?"

Heather opened her door. "I'm ready."

"Let's do this," Charlotte said.

"As ready as I'll ever be." Alice grimaced.

I scanned the parking lot. Jessica's red Jaguar was a few vehicles down. I hoped that meant that she was there this time. Jessica's car wasn't the only one I recognized. Dylan's police cruiser was in the lot too.

I nudged Heather. "Look who it is."

She followed my gaze. "I thought he wasn't talking to her until later?"

"That's what he said. Now what do we do?" I asked.

"You have to go talk to her anyway. Or at the least eavesdrop on the conversation between Jessica and Dylan," Charlotte said.

I could definitely do that. I would have a lot

of explaining to do if Dylan caught me. He'd probably tell me to stay out of the investigation. But I'd helped him, so could he really tell me to mind my own business?

We walked across the lawn toward the trailers. I kept an eye out for Dylan or Jessica. And I was watching out for the security guard too. I was pretty sure he was somewhere taking a nap. Why was he never guarding the place? Don't get me wrong, though—I was happy about that.

When we reached the trailer, it occurred to me that I could have the ghosts peek in and see if Jessica was there. No, that would have been bad. It wasn't very nice to invade someone's privacy like that . . . never mind that I'd done it. I knew all too well how that felt. I didn't want to encourage the ghosts to do it to someone else. I climbed the little metal stairs to the trailer and knocked. I just hoped Dylan wasn't in there talking with Jessica.

I held my breath as I waited for someone to answer, but no one did. I knocked again. Heather stood with the ghosts at the bottom of the stairs.

"She's not there again?" Heather asked.

"That's the way it looks," I said with frustration in my voice.

Maybe we'd have to hang out at her car or the trailer and wait for her to show up. She couldn't stay away forever. I stepped down to the bottom.

"What do we do now?" Heather asked.

"I guess we should just leave," Alice said.

"No way are we leaving now," Charlotte said.

I released a deep breath and looked around.

Still no security guard in sight. I could just walk into Jessica's trailer. What if I had been a stalker? What if it was Vera Lemon coming around to the actors' trailers?

"I should check again and see if anyone is in there." I motioned over my shoulder.

"Sure," Heather said. "I can watch out for you this time."

Okay, that meant I'd be going in alone. I moved up the steps to the door and knocked.

"Hello?" I called out.

When I twisted the doorknob, it opened.

I looked back at Heather and the ghosts. They were all standing guard, looking around. Heather and Charlotte gestured for me to go ahead. Alice just grimaced.

I stepped into Jessica's dressing room trailer. The door leading to the bedroom area was open. Maneuvering around a chair and a pair of red high heel shoes left on the floor, I tiptoed over and peeked inside. The bed was made, and the clothing had disappeared. I wondered where she'd put it. I stepped over to the closet and looked in. Nothing was hanging in there. Had she cleared out all of her belongings? Was she leaving?

I had to find her before she got out of town. We would have to go back to the lot and see if her car was still there. Maybe I needed to check around the set. Ask others if she had left. But then they might ask me why I was hanging around. I could just use the excuse that I was looking for the clothing. After all, I kind of was looking for it.

I was beginning to wonder if Shiloh was really going to return the clothing to me or if she was telling yet another lie. I had a lot of money tied up in those pieces, and several of them could not be replaced.

I hurried back outside. I caught movement up ahead and thought I saw Dylan. Whoever it was disappeared behind the trees and bushes.

"Did you see that?" I asked.

Heather and the ghosts snapped to attention.

"I think I just saw Dylan."

"Where?" Heather whipped around.

"Over there." I pointed. "But I can't be sure."

"We need to get out of here," Alice said.

While I didn't want Dylan to find me, I hadn't come this far to back off now. I was maybe actually onto something this time.

"We can't leave yet, I haven't talked to Jessica."

"I doubt you're going to find her," Charlotte said.

"Well, I have to try just a little more."

Maybe Wind Song knew something, after all. If Jessica had packed her bags, maybe she planned to get out of the state before she was caught. She could suspect that I was close to discovering that she'd killed Nicole.

"We should walk around and see if we can spot her. We can also check the parking lot and make sure her car is still there. I suspect she might be ready to skip town. All of her clothing is missing from the trailer," I said.

"Maybe she is moving in with Preston," Heather

said. She did have a point. Preston and Jessica had met at the hotel. Maybe they were taking the relationship to a new level.

"Let's walk over to the garden." I gestured for everyone to follow me.

"That's where I first saw Cookie." I heard Alice whisper to Charlotte.

It seemed like ages ago since our first encounter. My attention was on high alert as we crossed the lawn. This was where I'd seen the person I thought was Dylan.

We reached the garden area, but he wasn't there. Not that I could see anyway. Birds chirped in the trees, and a slight wind rustled the branches. It was one of the most peaceful places I'd ever been, a shady bower caressed by a cool breeze.

"Where do we go now?" Heather asked.

"I guess we can go up that path," I said. "We can head in the direction of the pond. I don't know where they are filming today. They could be in the main house. I doubt we'd make it past security for that."

"You're probably right. We have a lot of ground to cover," Heather said, releasing a deep breath.

We walked up the path toward the pond. Only a few white clouds dotted the sky, and the scent of jasmine carried across the air. The humidity made it like a sauna though. That wasn't anything new. It was always that way in Sugar Creek in summer.

I stopped and looked back.

"What's wrong?" Heather asked.

"I thought I heard something," I said.

"It was probably a squirrel," Charlotte answered.

I nodded. "Yes, you're right."

We had just turned to the left toward the pond when I spotted Vera. I grabbed Heather's arm and motioned with a tilt of my head. Heather spotted her too.

"What is she doing?" Heather whispered.

I shrugged. "I don't know, but we should find out."

Vera's back was to us, and she was walking at a snail's pace. Charlotte and Alice were still behind us.

"I just don't understand this woman. Why does she spend so much time sneaking over here?" Charlotte asked.

I supposed Vera could have asked the same thing about me. Vera reached a tall magnolia tree and stopped. Heather and I slipped behind a giant oak.

"Do you think she saw us?" Heather asked.

"I don't think so. What is she doing?" I asked Charlotte and Alice.

"She appears to be spying on someone," Charlotte answered.

"That is weird. I wonder who she's watching." I peeked out from behind the oak and saw Vera move to a tulip poplar. I motioned for Heather to walk with me. "We have to keep track of her. I don't want her to get away."

First we had been looking for Jessica, but now I couldn't let Vera out of my sight.

"We need to find out who she's spying on," Heather said.

"That could be tricky," I said. "If we get close enough to see who it is, she'll probably notice us. A confrontation with Vera is the last thing we need. I experienced that once and it wasn't pleasant."

Alice marched forward. "Oh, for goodness' sake, I will go and see who she's watching. You all stay put."

Heather and I exchanged a look.

"I can't figure that woman out either," Charlotte said.

Alice glided off. We watched as she stood next to Vera. I had a feeling she wouldn't leave without having a little fun. Alice turned around, but before leaving, she yanked the hat from Vera's head and threw it on the ground. Vera looked at the trees and all around to find the reason for her hat flying off. I hid behind the oak again so she wouldn't see me. Alice popped up beside us again.

"So who was it?" I asked.

"She was watching Preston."

"Alice, that wasn't very nice what you did to Vera."

"Sorry," she said without looking the least bit remorseful. "I just couldn't help myself."

I peeked out at Vera again. "I wonder why she is watching him. Is she stalking him too, like she did Nicole?"

"It could be something she just started," Heather said.

Preston walked away from the area, and Vera stepped back to hide behind the tulip poplar. Of course Heather and I did the same thing. Preston walked down the path without noticing us.

Once he had disappeared from sight, Vera walked in the opposite direction. She glanced back again, and I hid.

"This is making me a nervous wreck," Charlotte said. "I can't handle this kind of stress. If I wasn't already dead it would kill me."

I peeked out again. Vera was walking again, but I never knew when she would stop and look back. I didn't want her to spot us.

"If we stay over here by these bushes, we should be able to follow Vera without her noticing us." I pointed toward a clump of forsythia.

Heather agreed. "Okay. Let's give it a go."

We inched forward, making sure to stay quiet.

We were near the tree where Vera had been hiding when I noticed something on the ground.

"Look at that." I pointed.

Heather picked it up. "It's a tarot card."

Chapter 22

*Don't forget my all-time favorite way
to capture a living person's attention:
turning lights on and off.
That just never gets old.*

"Well, I'll be," Charlotte said.

"What is that woman up to?" Alice said.

Why would Vera have a tarot card? It had to be hers, right? Was it from the same set as the cards that had been left at my shop? I couldn't wait to find out.

Heather handed me the card. I flipped it over and saw that the design was the same as the ones that had been left in my store while I was locked in the back room.

"There is something fishy going on," Charlotte said.

"And it's not the smell coming from that pond either," Alice said.

"What does this card mean?" I asked Heather. She took the card from my outstretched hand. The card featured an angel wearing a light blue gown and burgundy-colored wings. "It's the judgment card. Meaning a day of reckoning. It's tied to the justice card."

"So this card fits with the rest of them?" I said.

"Yes, very much so," Heather said.

"Oh, this isn't good." Alice twisted her hands.

"So this could be for me? Maybe she planned on leaving it with the other cards?"

Heather winced. "It's possible."

"I wonder if there are more cards around here that she lost."

"Did she lose it?" Charlotte asked. "Or drop it on purpose?"

That was a good question that I didn't have an answer for. Heather and I walked around the tulip poplar tree scanning the area.

"I don't see any more cards," Heather said.

I pushed the hair out of my eyes. "Me either."

If Vera had left the card, then how did she get it in the first place?

"Did Vera buy a set of these cards too?" I asked Heather.

"Definitely not," she said. "At least, not from

me. I would have remembered her coming into the store."

"She is a memorable character," Charlotte said.

Heather handed the card back to me. I stuffed it in my pocket so that I could show Dylan. Although again I would have to explain how I just happened to find it. Who was I kidding? He knew I was snooping around. There was no use hiding it.

"Vera could have stolen the cards from Jessica," Heather pointed out.

I pondered this idea. "Yes, she could have, but when? Was it after Jessica left the cards at my shop? Or before the cards were left at my shop? That would mean Vera had left them there. Then again, it could be neither one of them."

"Those cards have seen a lot of traveling," Alice said.

"We have no way of knowing. Let's walk to the edge of the property," I said.

"Why, so she can catch you?" Charlotte asked.

"I'm not sure that's a good idea," Alice added.

"Vera could be waiting for us over there," Heather said.

"All of you are thinking like chickens. We have to be tough and stand up to Vera, remember?" Who was I to tell them not to be afraid? I had been scared of Vera too.

Heather puffed her chest out. "You're right, Cookie. Let's show her a thing or two."

"This probably won't end well," Alice said.

"It rarely does, dear," Charlotte said.

My companions followed me up the small hill and across the yard toward the edge of the plantation. I wouldn't deny that I was nervous about this whole mess. But I decided to be strong and push forward. We'd just reached the edge of the property, and I hadn't seen Vera again, when I spotted the security guard.

"Uh-oh, it looks like we got trouble."

"See, I told you it rarely ends well," Charlotte said to Alice.

"Is he looking this way?" Heather asked.

"Not yet. But we should hide again in case he's looking for us."

"Even if he's not looking for you, if he sees you he will throw your tushies out." Charlotte waved her hands.

"Vera could have seen us and called the police. I wouldn't put it past her at all," Alice said.

We scampered across the lawn again to a boxwood hedge that lent its fragrance to the heavy atmosphere. I tried to catch my breath. It was crazy that we had to hide from people. Maybe the guard wouldn't have said anything to us at all. After all, I had brought the pass that they had given me.

Movement came from behind us, and I held my breath. Heather looked at me with wide eyes. The guard was probably going to reach out and grab us. But after a few seconds, he walked on past. Like Preston, he never even looked in our direction.

When he was out of sight, I said, "That was a close one. I thought for sure he was going to grab us."

"Me too," Heather said.

"Ladies, you all are bananas," Charlotte said.

"You're just as crazy as we are, Charlotte. After all, you're here with us too," I said.

"Touché," she said.

Alice laughed.

"Did she call us crazy? She's one to talk," Heather shooed away a fly.

"Okay, let's not argue. We have to figure out what we're doing."

"I know what we should do," Alice said.

"What's that?" I asked.

"Leave." Her expression remained completely serious.

I frowned. "Not the plan I wanted to hear."

Male voices carried across the hot summer air from behind us. Surprisingly, I recognized both of them. It was Preston Hart and Ken Harrington, but I couldn't quite make out what they were saying.

"It's Preston and the lawyer," I said.

Charlotte and Alice both popped out from behind the boxwoods to get a better look.

"I wish I could hear what they are talking about." I looked at Charlotte and Alice to give them a not-so-subtle hint.

"Hint taken," Charlotte said as she glided away.

Alice trailed behind her.

"They're going to eavesdrop," I said.

Heather clapped her hands. "Great."

The ghosts hadn't even reached the men when they ended their conversation. Preston turned to his left, and Ken turned to his right.

Charlotte and Alice reappeared beside us. "Sorry, no luck this time," Charlotte said.

"That's okay. Things aren't working out as well as I'd hoped," I said.

I looked at Heather. "We should get out of here."

"What about finding Jessica?" she asked.

"It looks like that is a lost cause."

"Sadly, I think you're right," Charlotte said.

"I wish we'd found out what Preston and Ken were talking about. It probably had something to do with the case," I said.

"You should tell Preston that Vera was watching him. That would probably scare the khaki pants off him. I bet he gets that kind of thing all the time," Charlotte said.

"It would be tough to deal with," Alice said.

I stepped away from the hedge and brushed off my clothing. Maybe my vintage outfit wasn't great to chase after people in. I hoped I didn't ruin it.

Heather leaned out for a look. "Everyone is gone."

We left our hiding spot and followed the path that wound around the pond. I avoided looking at the spot where I'd seen Nicole.

We turned toward the car. Walking across the perfectly manicured lawn seemed somehow wrong, but there was no other way to reach the parking lot.

"I can't believe we never found Jessica," Heather said.

"I bet she's already gone by now. She's probably at the airport in Atlanta and preparing to get on a plane." I weaved around another boxwood.

"Don't say that. There is no way we can go to Atlanta and find Jessica in the busiest airport ever."

I had to accept her logic. "No, you're right. That was a crazy thought. Besides, we don't even know if that was where she was going."

When we reached the edge of the parking lot, Jessica was heading toward her car.

"There she is," Charlotte called out.

Heather and I stopped behind a white minivan.

"What do we do now?" I whispered.

"Go talk to her," Heather said. "Isn't that what we came here to do?"

"Please just be careful," Alice said with worry in her voice.

We inched closer to Jessica's car. She had a couple of suitcases in her hands. She stopped at the back of her car and placed the bags on the ground.

"Looks like she packed her bags," Heather said.

Just then rain started to pour from the sky, pounding against the pavement. It was one of those summer cloudbursts that struck without warning. We were getting drenched.

"Oh my gosh, I can't believe it's raining," I said. "My shoes are going to be ruined."

Jessica looked up at the sky and cussed. The clouds were spotty, and it looked as if it wasn't even raining in the near distance. I hoped it didn't last long.

Jessica fumbled with her keys, trying to get the trunk to unlock. It looked as if her remote wasn't working. The rain was beating down on all of us. Except, it was having no effect on the ghosts. They still looked just as perfect as they always had.

Despite the rain we stood there and watched her.

"I'm soaking," Heather said.

"Well, don't just stand there. Go talk to her. You've found her and that's what you wanted to do. You're just wasting time at this point," Charlotte said.

I had to make my move. I hadn't thought about what to say exactly. So I guessed I would just wing it.

Jessica had gotten the trunk open and was tossing the bags around inside it. When one wouldn't fit, she slammed it onto the ground. Her blond hair was plastered to her head. She grabbed a Vuitton carry-on and threw it in the trunk for another attempt on making it fit. This time she got it in. She slammed the trunk down and ran around the side of the car.

Turning the corner too sharp, Jessica fell on her bottom on the wet pavement. She cussed and struggled to push to her feet.

"Oh, that is not very ladylike," Charlotte said.

I pushed the wet hair from my forehead and

pushed my shoulders back. "Okay, we need to confront her now."

"Right," Heather said.

Yet we stood in the same spot, letting the rain pound down on us.

"If you don't go over there right now, I will haunt you for the rest of your life." Charlotte's voice reminded me of the high school principal reprimanding us for being late to class.

"Me too," Alice threatened.

Heather followed me as we moved across the lot and closer to Jessica. I glanced over to make sure my Buick was okay. It was a good thing that I'd left the top up.

Jessica had gotten up and reached the driver's side door. Heather and I picked up the pace. Jessica dropped her keys. I wasn't sure if she was always this clumsy or if something was making her nervous.

When Jessica picked up her keys, she looked up and spotted us. She glared at us but remained frozen on the spot.

"What is she going to do?" Alice asked.

I didn't answer as I focused my full attention on Jessica.

"I think she's going to jump in her car and take off, leaving you standing there like a couple of bumps on a log," Charlotte said.

I wasn't about to let Jessica get away. I guess I could get in my car and go after her. Would her Jaguar beat my Buick? I had no idea.

"I'd say by the look on her face she is really mad too," Charlotte added.

Jessica moved to her right, toward my car now. She wasn't going to let us get out of here, I realized.

"Well, we're two against one," Heather said.

"What if she has a gun or some other weapon?" I asked.

"That would change things dramatically." Heather didn't take her eyes off Jessica.

"I think we should get out of here," I said out of the corner of my mouth.

"Where are we going?" Heather asked.

"Away from Jessica," I said.

We turned around and took off over the lawn. It was hard to keep my footing in the wet grass. I tried my best to keep from falling, but I wasn't sure how long I would win that battle. When I looked back, I saw that Jessica was running after us.

Charlotte and Alice were gliding along at our side.

"Why are you running? It's two against one, remember?" Charlotte said.

"Yes, but she looks crazy. It's better if we get away from her," I said as I picked up speed.

"I've never seen a look in anyone's eyes like that before," Heather said, panting.

"I've seen it before. When I confronted Charlotte's killer," I said.

"Oh yeah, that was bad," Charlotte said.

I glanced over my shoulder. Jessica was gaining on us.

Heather was wheezing for breath. "We need to hurry."

"Maybe going to confront Jessica wasn't such a good idea after all," Charlotte said.

"I tried to tell you all that it wasn't such a good idea. But you wouldn't listen to me. No, you had to do it anyway. Maybe next time you will listen to me when I tell you something." Exasperation filled Alice's voice.

"Alice, this is not the time to say 'I told you so.'" Adrenaline rushed through me as I pushed to run faster.

"You might as well stop. I'll catch you," Jessica called out.

Chapter 23

Cookie's Savvy Vintage Fashion Shopping Tips

*Bring cash when you go shopping as some
stores may not accept credit cards or checks.*

This wasn't looking good.

"Maybe if we act like we don't hear her she will
go away?" Heather asked.

"Something tells me that won't make a difference.
If anything, it would probably make her angrier."

"Why don't you just stop and simply explain to
her that you just want to go to your car and that
you don't want any trouble?" Charlotte asked.

"Did you see the look in her eyes? I think she'd
kill us if we did that. Let's just keep going," I said.

We had almost reached the pond again. I had
grass and mud on my shoes. The lawn wasn't so
neat anymore. When we reached the path, we
would have to decide which way to turn. I thought
it would be best to go toward the plantation. There
were other houses and even a small cottage in the

other direction. But it would be more likely that the crew was at the plantation.

I glanced back and saw Jessica right behind us.

"You might as well stop," she said.

She was right. I looked at Heather, and we both turned around at the same time.

Jessica placed her hands on her hips and glared at me. Her hair was wet and stuck to her face. Black mascara had run down her cheeks.

Of course my makeup probably looked the same.

"Hello, Jessica. We were just getting ready to leave. I hadn't expected the rain." I pointed at the sky.

"You're really talking about the weather? Ask her if she killed Nicole," Charlotte said.

"She can't just come out and ask that," Alice said.

Jessica squinted. "Why are you spying on me? What's your name? Are you Cookie?"

She knew perfectly well what my name was. She knew where my shop was too.

"Yes, my name is Cookie, and no, we weren't spying on you."

She arched a perfectly sculpted eyebrow. "Then why were you and your pal hiding behind that minivan and peeking at me?"

"Like I said, we were just going to leave. You just happened to be in the parking lot at the time."

I had to let her know that I wasn't going to be afraid of her anymore. It was the only way to get out of this situation. I decided to go on the offensive.

"Did you get a set of tarot cards from Shiloh?"

She scoffed. "I don't think so."

I knew by the look in her eyes that she was lying.

"Shiloh gave you the cards and you left some of them in my shop. You did that on purpose to send me a message, right? And you locked me in the back room?"

If I was falsely accusing her, then this would be awkward, but I had a feeling that I was right on track.

"Keep up the questions, Cookie. I think you're getting to her," Charlotte said.

"You are crazy," Jessica said. "What makes you think I would do something like that?" Her voice sounded more anxious than before.

I pressed on.

"What about the text messages that you sent to Nicole?"

She studied my face. The black mascara really gave her a spooky look. "What are you talking about?"

"The messages that you sent to Nicole. You told her that you wanted the lead role for this movie. I found her phone," I said.

"You took it?" Jessica asked.

"No, I found it."

She narrowed her eyes. "You will not get away with this. I tried to give you a warning. I figured your friend would see the meaning of the cards and tell you to back off. But you didn't listen. I told you I would get revenge. You had to keep coming around here. I saw you poking around. You wouldn't mind your own business."

I realized she was confessing to me.

"You had the cards wrong," Heather said. "That wasn't their actual meaning. That was how we knew it was a novice who left them. We figured out that Shiloh had stolen the cards."

Jessica clenched her fists. "I should have known not to take something from her. She's constantly taking things. Both of you will pay for this," Jessica snapped.

"I'm going for help," Heather said.

"You won't find any help around here. The security guard is always sleeping. You'll never find his secret spot."

Heather took off running down the path. "Cookie, I'll go get help."

Jessica laughed. "Oh, that is so sweet. She is going to help her friend. When she comes back with no help she'll find you dead and then I will kill her."

Chills ran down my spine.

"My heavens, I've never heard anyone so evil," Alice said.

She was right. Jessica was evil. I had to get away from her. If only I hadn't left my phone in the car. I hoped Heather remembered that it was there. She could call for help. That was when I remembered that the car was locked. And Heather, most likely, had forgotten to charge her battery.

There would be no way she could call for help. I would have to get away from Jessica.

"Why did you kill Nicole? Couldn't you have

just gotten a part in another movie? Was it really worth killing her?"

"She was with Preston too. She had it all. My roles and my man."

Oh, I'd forgotten about her involvement with Preston.

"Now that she is gone I don't have to worry about her taking my parts or my man."

I felt bad for the next actress who won a part over Jessica. She would try to kill her too. She had to be stopped.

"You had Nicole's phone and lost it here when you came back to the scene of the crime, didn't you? You wanted to come back here so you could relive what you'd done, right?" I asked.

She glared at me and I knew my assumptions were correct.

Jessica reached out and grabbed the sleeve of my dress. It happened so fast I didn't have time to move. Wiggling like a crazy eel, I managed to pull away.

"We can't let her do this," Alice said.

"I don't know how to stop her," Charlotte said.

I stepped backward, trying to put distance between Jessica and me. She moved toward me with every step I took. I slipped in the wet grass but managed to right myself.

We crossed over the path and back onto the grassy area.

"Cookie, look out," Alice yelled.

"Behind you," Charlotte shouted.

When I turned around, I realized that I was by

the water. Was this how she'd killed Nicole? Would I end up with the same fate?

"Don't let her get you," Charlotte called out.

I was trying my best, but Jessica was tough. She was much stronger than she looked.

"Oh, I can't watch. All the negative vibes are snapping my energy," Alice said.

I moved forward. I'd only made it one step when Jessica grabbed me again. I was so very close to the edge of the water. I was just an okay swimmer. I didn't know how deep the water was. Jessica would probably hold me under. I hoped Heather didn't come back. I didn't want Jessica to attack her too.

I pulled my arms up and managed to spin Jessica. Now she was the one on the edge. Just a little more and I might be able to push her in. That might allow me time to get away. She had her hands on my arms, but her grip wasn't nearly as tight as it had been. Was she getting tired? I knew I was, but I couldn't give up now.

I pushed Jessica, but it wasn't enough to get her in the water.

"Keep going, Cookie, you almost had her," Charlotte shouted.

Jessica's sandal was now stuck in the mud at the edge of the pond. Our eyes met. She looked panicked.

"You've got her right where you want her now," Alice said.

"Give her a shove."

I pulled away, gasping.

"You won't get away with this. Get back here and help me," Jessica said.

Yeah, right. Did she think I was that stupid? Trying to keep as much distance between us as possible, I reached over and shoved Jessica. She stumbled backward, trying to right herself with the aid of her arms. But it was no use—she fell backward. A large splash rose up when she hit the water.

"Good job, Cookie, now get away from her." Charlotte didn't have to tell me; I was already moving across the path.

When I looked back, I realized that Jessica had gotten the shoe off.

"Uh-oh, here she comes," Alice said.

Jessica had managed to get out of the water. She looked even angrier now. I was in trouble if I couldn't get out of there.

"Run, Cookie," Charlotte urged.

I took off across the lawn, trying not to slip. I wish I had time to stop and take my shoes off. I could move faster without them, but I couldn't afford to stop. I was headed in the direction of the parking lot. If I could just make it to my car, I could use the phone.

Jessica slowed down because her feet were slipping. I moved my legs as fast as I could until I felt they would fall off. My side hurt, and it was difficult to catch my breath.

A hand grabbed my shoulder, and I fell to the ground. Jessica had caught up to me. I struggled to my feet. Jessica got up at the same time. She reached to grab my arm yet again. She just wasn't going to give up. I saw the hate in her eyes.

"You aren't getting away," Jessica said.

I was going to try my best to get away, that was for sure.

"Let her have it," Charlotte said.

Jessica swung at me with her other hand, and I managed to duck. Now she was throwing punches. My daddy had taught me a thing or two about fist fighting. I just needed to land a good one on her jaw. Jessica still had a hold of my left arm. But that left my right arm free. So I pulled back my arm and punched forward with all that I had. My fist landed squarely on her jaw. My daddy would be proud to see that I'd used what he'd taught me. I yanked my arm away and spun around.

When I took off, I ran smack-dab into someone's hard chest. I knew it was a man. I looked up into Dylan's eyes. Was I ever glad to see him. I stumbled forward, and he helped me right myself. He had a firm grip on my arms until I got my balance again. I wasn't sure how he'd found me, but I was thankful. And I didn't care if I had to explain why I was there. He would just have to deal with it.

He looked me in the eyes, but didn't say anything.

When I was on my feet, he yelled out at Jessica. "Stop right there." He pulled his gun and pointed.

She was frozen on the spot. But it didn't look as if she was quite ready to turn herself in just yet.

"Oh, thank goodness he is here," Alice said.

"My nerves couldn't have handled much more of that," Charlotte said.

Jessica didn't stop like Dylan had told her to. Instead, she turned around and ran. Dylan took off after her. He was much faster than she was, and I knew it would be a matter of seconds until he caught up to her.

Just as I knew he would, Dylan caught up to her, giving her shoulder a hard shove. She fell to the ground, and he grabbed her up, bringing her to her feet.

"You're hurting me," she said.

Yeah, she hadn't been too worried about hurting Nicole or me. Besides, he wasn't hurting her.

"Thank goodness this is over," Charlotte said.

"You're going to jail," Alice said.

I released a deep breath. Where was Heather? Had she been the one to find Dylan? Now I was worried about what had happened to her.

Dylan put Jessica in handcuffs and spun her around. "Come on. We're going for a ride."

He walked Jessica across the lawn.

"Are you okay?" he asked.

"Yes, I'm fine. But we need to find Heather. She could be in danger." I hoped Dylan understood the seriousness of the situation.

"I'll look for her after I secure this suspect," he said. I followed Dylan as he led Jessica toward the parking lot.

Chapter 24

*Charlotte's Handy-Dandy Tips
for Navigating the Afterlife*

*Opening and slamming doors
is the classic haunting antic.
This tried-and-true method
will always get results.*

We arrived at the parking lot as other police cars showed up. Jessica wasn't talking to the cops. She looked over her shoulder a few times to glare at me. Dylan put her in his car until the other officers came to get her. I was shocked to see that the news crew from Savannah had shown up. I hid behind my car, hoping that I could avoid an interview.

"It would be good advertising for the store," Charlotte urged.

That was true, but I wasn't sure about that kind of publicity. Besides, I was a soaking wet mess.

The ambulance arrived, and Dylan insisted

that I get checked out. Of course, the paramedic confirmed what I already knew. It was just a couple of cuts and bruises. But I was worried about finding Heather. I knew that she should have returned by now. The knot in my stomach told me that something was wrong.

As soon as the paramedics were through with me, I had to go look for her. I could see that Dylan couldn't help me find her. He had too much going on at the moment.

Preston Hart came over and caught my arm.

"Hey, Cookie," he said. "What is going on? I can't get anybody to tell me what happened. Do you know?"

Did I ever. I had a front-row seat for all the action. But could I trust Preston? I still wasn't sure that he hadn't been involved. I would test him to see how he acted.

"Jessica is the one who killed Nicole." I looked at him for a reaction.

He swayed as if he would fall over. "Are you serious?"

Okay, it appeared that it had come as a shock, but then again, he was an actor.

"What happened?"

"She attacked me down by the water when I asked her about it. She admitted it to me."

"I find that hard to believe," he said.

Was he calling me a liar? I shrugged. "Well, it's the truth and my friend heard her too."

"Not to mention the ghosts," Charlotte said.

"Where are they taking Jessica?" He pointed toward Dylan's police car.

"To jail," I said.

"So this is real?" he asked.

"Very much so, I'm afraid."

"Why would she kill Nicole?" he asked.

"Jessica said Nicole stole the part in this movie from her. And also that Nicole stole you. I guess Jessica thinks that you are a couple. Is that true? Were you dating her?" I asked.

"No way. I was not dating her. She was supposed to be my friend. She was supposed to be Nicole's friend too," he said. "How could a friend do something like this?"

"Well, obviously, she wasn't really a friend."

Preston leaned against my car and placed his head in his hands. Now I truly believed that he hadn't been involved. He really seemed upset by the news. Not only had he lost his fiancée, but someone he thought was a friend had taken Nicole from him.

But I still hadn't gotten the answer for one thing.

"I saw you at the Plaza Hotel with Jessica," I said. "You met her in the lobby and then went upstairs. You were holding hands."

He looked up, red-eyed. "I thought she needed comforting. I know I did and I figured she did too. My parents had arrived in town that day and I took her up to meet them. Not that I have to explain this to you, but there was nothing going on between us."

He was right. He didn't owe me an explanation.

"Preston, I am sorry about your loss. I hate that I had to be the one to tell you about Jessica. I know it can hurt deeply when you find out that a friend has betrayed you."

He stared straight ahead, lost in thought. "Thank you for the information. I hope you're doing okay."

"Thanks. I'm fine." I nodded.

"Well, I'd better go," he said.

He didn't get far before a police officer stopped him. As I scanned the area again, I realized that all of the movie crew was now standing around. Charlotte and Alice stood beside me, taking in all the excitement.

"Hey, what is she doing?" I followed Charlotte's pointing finger to see what she was talking about. Apparently, Dylan had taken Jessica from the backseat of his car to transfer her over to the vehicle that would take her to jail. She was moving her arms and hands a lot. No one was paying attention to her. The police officer who was supposed to be watching her was talking to someone else. The next thing I knew, Jessica had slipped her hands out of the cuffs.

"What was she doing? I can't believe she did that," Alice said.

"I've seen it happen before on TV," Charlotte said. "She probably has small hands."

I had to catch someone's attention before Jessica got away. I was afraid that she would try to grab the policeman's gun. Instead, she decided to take off running.

I waved my arms through the air, trying to get anyone's attention. I called to Dylan, but my voice didn't carry over the noise of so many people talking.

I took off across the lot, rushing toward a group of officers. I hoped they didn't think I was trying to attack them. What did I have to do to get someone's attention around here? Jessica had already made it to the edge of the parking lot. Soon she would be on Vera's property. If I were Jessica, I would rather take my chances with the police taking me to jail. Vera would freak out if Jessica stepped on her land. Dylan finally looked over and noticed me.

I gestured toward Jessica, but he thought I was motioning to his car. He smiled. This wasn't going as well as I'd hoped. Couldn't he just see what I was pointing at? Jessica was about to slip through their fingers. I pointed out Jessica to Dylan. Once again he waved, but then looked over his shoulder. That was when he must have seen her.

Dylan set out, running after Jessica. When the other officers realized what had happened, they took off in a sprint too.

"She is one gutsy sociopath," Charlotte said. "She's as slippery as a snake."

The cops were yelling at Jessica to stop, but she wasn't about to listen. They would have to tackle her. Jessica had paused to take off her sandals and tossed them to the side.

Dylan was the first one who reached her. He grabbed her and brought her down with one big swoop. She landed on the ground, and he was almost on top of her. I couldn't hear what was said because I was too far away, but I figured she was complaining that he was hurting her again. The other officers reached them as Dylan pulled her to her feet while holding her arms behind her back. She looked far from the movie star, with the crazy hair, smudged makeup, and dirty clothes. The tabloids would love photos of her like this.

Reporters and photographers clamored behind the yellow crime scene tape. They were snapping photos of Jessica as Dylan escorted her back across the lot. He took her over to the police car, and another officer added cuffs around her ankles. She was complaining the whole time. Dylan opened the backseat door, and then shoved her in.

"She would have to be Houdini to break out of those foot cuffs," Charlotte said.

"She is really strong," Alice said with wide eyes.

Dylan walked over to me.

He took my hand. "Good eyes."

I might have blushed just a little.

"I can't believe they almost let her get away like that. If you hadn't been watching, then she probably would have succeeded. We need to have you on the police force."

He smiled.

I tried to find my voice. "It was nothing, really."

Charlotte coughed from over my shoulder. I ignored her.

"Well, thanks again." He slid his hand up my arm. It was then that I remembered how awful I must look with the streaked makeup and dirty clothing. Oddly enough, Dylan didn't seem to care what I looked like.

"I guess I'd better get back over there." He gestured over his shoulder. "I'll be back in just a few."

I wanted to tell him about Heather, but didn't have the chance. While Dylan was talking to the officers, I decided I would take matters into my own hands once again and look for my friend.

I slipped away back onto the plantation's lawn. I figured that Heather had gone in the direction of the main house, so I would look there first. I tried not to worry, but that wasn't easy. Maybe she had just gotten turned around and couldn't find her way back.

The area seemed isolated now that everyone had gathered down at the parking lot because of the police activity. I reached the massive house, with its white columns and giant porch. I marched up the steps toward the front door. I had no idea why Heather would still be inside if this was in fact where she'd gone for help, but since I didn't see her, I had to check inside. I stepped up to the big black door and knocked. Why was I knocking? No one was there to answer.

I twisted the doorknob, and the door opened. I

stepped inside the massive foyer of the home. The hardwood floors glistened under my feet. It appeared that the house was empty.

"Hello?" I called out.

My voice echoed through the large foyer. As I inched my way inside, I saw that a couple of wooden benches lined the walls. A crystal chandelier dangled above me. The rooms on each side of me were decorated with ornate period furniture. I walked from room to room, but saw no one.

It was strange to be inside the house when no one else was around. I had wanted to see the place, but not under these circumstances. I'd only gotten a chance to see the outside until now.

"Heather, are you in here?" I called out. I moved through every room downstairs, hoping that I wouldn't get lost. The place was so big it would be easy to do. I'd moved through the kitchen and back to the foyer and still no sign of her.

I turned to my left to head up the stairs when I heard what I thought sounded like footsteps. My heart rate increased, and I didn't know if I should call out again. I was still a little panicked over what had happened with Jessica. Sure, the police had cuffed even her feet this time, but a little voice in the back of my head said, "What if she got out again and is coming for you?" The sound continued through the room to my right, and I wondered if I should find a place to hide.

I hurried to my left and pulled on the first door that I came to. My intent was to hide in there until whoever was in the house went away. I'd peek out and make sure it wasn't Heather. But if it was her, wouldn't she have answered me when I called out to her?

My hand was on the doorknob when a male voice called out, "Cookie? What are you doing in here?"

I froze on the spot. I knew that I had to turn around. I eased around to see who had called out to me.

Ken Harrison, the attorney, stood in the foyer with a puzzled look on his face. "Are you lost?"

I closed the door and faced him. "I'm looking for Heather," I said. "She went to get help for us and I haven't seen her since."

Now that I thought of it, what was he doing in the house when everyone else was outside?

"You do know about what happened?" I asked.

"Yes, I'm sorry that happened to you. I'm glad they finally got the person who harmed Nicole. I knew Preston was innocent the whole time."

I wished I could say the same thing. But I had suspected him.

"Thank you." I glanced down at my dirty outfit.

"Speaking of Preston," Ken said. "Have you seen him? I've been looking all over for him."

So that was why he was in here. He was looking for someone too. "Actually, I saw him down at the parking lot. I believe the police had a few questions for him."

He ran a hand through his hair. "He should have called me."

"I guess you'd better get down there to him." I motioned toward Preston.

"I can help you find Heather first."

I waved him off. "No, that won't be necessary. I'm sure she's around here somewhere." My voice didn't sound confident about that.

"Come on, let me help you look around. I'm sure that we'll spot her soon. I won't take no for an answer." He smiled, and dimples appeared on his cheeks.

How could I refuse a look like that? Plus, the help would be nice.

"That is so sweet that he wants to help you," Alice said.

"You should let him," Charlotte added.

"Okay, if you insist." I couldn't hide the worry in my voice.

He looked pleased. "I do."

"I already looked downstairs. Should we look up there?" I asked.

"I can take a quick look around if you'd like."

"Sure, if you really don't mind."

Ken hurried up the stairs.

"He really is a cutie," Charlotte said.

"Yeah, you said that once before."

"I think it needed to be repeated," Alice said.

Charlotte laughed.

"I'm glad you all are having fun. I'm worried about Heather."

"She's fine. Don't worry so much. You'll find her," Charlotte said.

Ken came back down the grand staircase. "Did you say something?"

I shook my head. "No, why?"

"I thought I heard voices."

I cut a glance to Charlotte. "No, I didn't hear anything."

He must have overheard me talking to Charlotte and Alice.

A faint sound echoed across the foyer.

"Did you hear that?" Ken asked.

I stood still as if that would allow me to hear the sound better next time. "Yes, I did. It sounded like it came from that room or maybe outside."

Ken raced over to the parlor and peered inside the room. "No one is in here." The sound came again. It was like someone was moving something large or struggling to pull something.

"I really think it's coming from outside," I said.

He motioned for me to follow him to the front door. "Let's go check it out."

I hurried to join him, with the ghosts right behind me. Once we reached the bottom of the steps, I wasn't sure where to look first.

"Where did the sound come from?" Ken asked.

"I think it was that way." I pointed to the left.

"Hmm. I thought it was on the right," he said. "How about we split up? You look that way and I'll go this way. We can meet back here?"

"Sure. See you in a second." I turned to my left and headed around the house

The ghosts were right beside me.

"I think you were right, Cookie. The sound came from the left," Charlotte said.

"I just hope that we find Heather and nothing is

wrong with her. Be on the lookout for her, okay?"
I asked.

I made my way all the way around the side of
the house. Considering the size of the place, it
wasn't a quick trip. I reached the backyard and
paused. There were even more trees and bushes
back here. Plenty of places for people to hide.
Maybe I'd heard a cat? A raccoon?

I shielded my hand over my eyes to block
the sun that had now popped out from behind
the clouds.

"Do you see anything?" I asked Alice and
Charlotte.

"Not a thing," Charlotte answered.

"I guess I should go around and meet Ken at the
front again. Apparently Heather isn't here."

"Maybe she's already back at your car waiting
for you," Alice said.

I sighed. "I sure hope so."

Just as I turned to leave, I noticed a piece of
paper by the peony bush across from us. I moved
closer—I knew what it was.

"Oh my," Charlotte said.

She recognized it too.

"What is it?" Alice asked.

I reached down and picked it up. "It's another
tarot card." I flipped it over. "And it's from the
same deck. I guess Jessica was out here too."

The card had a skeleton riding a horse with red
and orange flames in the background. It was one
of the scariest images I'd ever seen.

"Did she leave them on purpose or do you think she just lost them?" Charlotte asked.

"I guess she just lost them," I said.

I stuffed the card in my pocket since I didn't have Heather to tell me what it meant. I figured Ken was probably looking for me by now. I scanned the area to see if there were any more cards. I didn't see any, but I did notice something else. I rushed over and picked up the phone from the ground. I touched the screen, and it lit up.

"The battery is still charged," I said to Charlotte and Alice.

I clicked on the RECENT CALL icon and noticed right away that it was Heather's phone. I thought she'd left it in my car. Plus, I thought for sure that I'd locked the car. How did the phone get back here? Panic really set in now. I just knew that Heather was in trouble.

"Cookie, look over there."

I followed the direction of Alice's pointing finger. Relief fell over me. It was Heather, standing by a magnolia tree. She wasn't looking in my direction. What was she doing? She hadn't even noticed me. How had she gotten lost back here?

"What is she doing?" Charlotte asked.

"I don't know, but I need to find out," I said.

I rushed toward my friend. Charlotte and Alice ran after me, then passed me.

"Heather, I'm over here," I yelled out.

Heather didn't look over at me. It was as if she was ignoring me. Had I made her mad? Was she sick? Something seemed seriously off.

"Heather, it's me, Cookie," I called out again.

Finally, she looked over at me. I knew by the look in her eyes that something was terribly wrong. She motioned with a tilt of her head.

"I think she's telling you to go away," Charlotte said.

"Why would she do that?" I asked.

"I think she's in trouble," Charlotte said.

Heather motioned again, and that was when I realized that Vera Lemon stood beside her.

Chapter 25

Cookie's Savvy Vintage Fashion Shopping Tips

❧

Don't buy just because an item is cheap.
Ask yourself if you'll really use the garment.

She had a gun pointed at Heather.

"Oh, this is not happening," Charlotte said.

I was afraid it was all too real. What would I do now? I had no idea why Vera was holding Heather at gunpoint. Had she stepped on her property?

"Vera, what are you doing?" I asked. "Put the gun down before you hurt someone."

She shook her head. "No way."

"We are friends now, remember?" I said. "You invited me to your party. It was nice."

She snorted. "Yeah, right."

"Even I didn't believe that," Alice said.

Well, at least I'd tried.

"Vera Lemon, what are you doing?" Ken called out.

He was standing behind me.

She motioned with the gun. "Don't come any closer."

He held his hands up. "We're not coming any closer. Vera, you do know that we're not on your property, right?" he asked.

I guess everyone knew that she had a problem with that.

"I know you're not right now. That doesn't mean you haven't been," she said.

"It's okay now, Vera. We won't go on your property. I'm sure Heather won't do that either. Isn't that right, Heather?" Ken asked.

Heather managed to nod, but the fear was evident in her eyes.

"Why don't you tell us what the problem is and we'll see if we can't work it out," Ken said.

Vera glared at him, but didn't respond. I wondered if I could dial Heather's phone for help without Vera's noticing.

"I told her to stay off my property. But she didn't listen and now she will have to pay the price. I can't keep telling people. It has to stop here." Vera waved the gun.

She was so consumed in her rant that she didn't even notice that Ken had walked around and was now almost directly behind her. I just had to keep her attention focused on me so that she wouldn't see him.

"Vera, we already told you that we wouldn't do that anymore. We'll even buy you a fence to keep everyone out."

I'd tell her anything if it would keep her from using that gun.

"I don't want a fence on my property. Are you kidding? If I'd wanted that I would have done it years ago."

"If you don't like the movie crew, then why did you invite them to a party at your place?"

"I thought I could convince everyone to go away," she said.

Ken had stepped up behind her now. One wrong move, and Vera could use that gun on us.

"I don't think I can watch anymore," Alice said.

"Stay strong for Cookie," Charlotte said.

That was what I had to remind myself. Stay strong.

In one fluid movement, Ken reached out and grabbed Vera from behind. She yelled and struggled to get away from his tight grip. I hoped that gun didn't go off in the process. Ken yanked Vera's arm down, and the gun fell from her hand and hit the ground. Thank goodness it didn't go off. Heather ran over and grabbed the gun. She ran over to me, and I hugged her.

"Cookie, I thought I never would get away from her."

"It's over now. Thank goodness you're okay."

"Watch where you're pointing that thing," Charlotte warned.

Heather held the gun to her side.

"I was so worried about you," Heather said. "I wanted to get help and then I ran into Vera."

"I got away from Jessica and Dylan showed up. The police are here and have arrested her."

"Oh, thank heavens."

Ken was lying on top of the struggling Vera. "Don't forget about me. Can you call the police?" he asked.

"Oh yeah, I almost forgot." I pulled Heather's phone from my pocket and dialed Dylan's number. After a few rings, he picked up.

"Where are you?" he asked when he discovered it was me.

After I told him the incredible story, he said he would be over right away. In the meantime, Ken had to keep Vera from getting away. She was squirming like a fish on a hook, but he was a muscular guy.

When I hung up, Heather asked, "Where did you find my phone?"

"It was over here by the bushes. There was a tarot card too. I didn't know that you'd lost your phone," I said.

"Yeah, earlier I couldn't find it. I have no idea how it got back there. You said you found cards back here too?" Heather asked.

I pointed toward the bush where I'd found the card. "Just one. It was right over there." I pulled it out of my pocket. "What is this card?" I handed it to her.

"It's the anger card."

Vera saw us and shouted, "Glad you found those cards. I took them from Jessica. She shouldn't have them anyway. She didn't deserve to take the role from Nicole."

"You took these cards from Jessica?" I asked.

"Well, I didn't take them. She dropped them. I picked up the ones she'd dropped. I guess I lost a couple too."

"That is one of the craziest things I've ever heard," Alice said. "I can't believe this woman."

"She makes me so angry," Charlotte said.

"Cookie, I'm here," Dylan called out.

I spun around.

"Heather, why do you have that gun?" Dylan asked.

"This was Vera's." She placed it on the ground.

Ken still had Vera pinned. She'd stopped fighting him now. Dylan rushed over to Ken and pulled cuffs from his back pocket.

"I'm going to need to bring more of these with me if this keeps up," he said as he secured Vera's hands.

After reading Vera her rights, Dylan asked, "Vera, do you want to explain to me what happened?"

"I told her to stay off my land."

"I wasn't even on her land," Heather said in frustration.

"Is that what this is about? Vera, when will you learn?"

"I guess I'll learn when everyone else learns to stay off my land."

Dylan nodded. "Okay, we'll talk about this at the police station."

To Ken he said, "Thanks for taking care of this."

"Anything for Cookie," Ken said with a smile.

Dylan stared for a beat and then turned toward me. I probably blushed when Ken and Dylan looked at me. Girlfriend to the rescue, Heather chose that moment to say, "Cookie, can you help me? I think I have something in my eye."

"I think both men are interested you, Cookie," Charlotte said with a snicker of delight.

Dylan walked Vera back across the lawn.

"Vera, you should be ashamed for your behavior," Charlotte said as if Vera could hear her.

"I'll take her down to the police car," Dylan said when he grew near.

"I'll be right there," I said.

Dylan glanced back at Ken and then continued walking.

When Ken walked over, he asked, "What happened, Heather?"

"When I came back toward the plantation, Vera spotted me. She pulled out the gun, so I had no choice but to go with her."

"What do you mean 'go with her'? Where did she take you?" I asked.

"She made me walk over toward her property so that she could show me the exact property line."

My mouth probably fell open. "I can't believe she did that."

Ken shook his head. "That is crazy. So then what happened?" he asked.

"When she finished, we came back over here. She wanted to find you, Cookie, so that she could bring you back over and show you the property lines."

"Oh, for heaven's sake, that is ridiculous."

"I'm just glad that you came along when you did." Heather looked down at my outfit. "What happened to you, by the way?"

"Jessica and I got into a little bit of a fight." I attempted to brush more dirt from my shirt, but it was no use. It would take some serious work to get these stains out.

"You should tell them how you really let Jessica have it," Charlotte said.

"She did have a good punch, huh?" Alice said.

I was glad Ken and Heather couldn't hear the ghosts because they were embarrassing me. I guess I had really given Jessica a run for her money though. I hated fighting, but sometimes you have to fight to survive. Jessica had probably underestimated me because of my petite size.

"Ken sure is handsome."

Heather and Ken were talking, and I had to listen to Charlotte and Alice.

"Why don't you ask him out?" Charlotte asked.

"I can't do that," I said out of the corner of my mouth.

"Who are you talking to?" Ken asked, looking over at me.

I waved off his question. "Oh, I was just muttering about my ruined clothing."

He gave me a little smile. "You still look great."

"See, he likes you," Charlotte continued.

"You know, I could have sworn I heard voices in the house. Are you sure you weren't talking to someone?"

I tried to act innocent. He couldn't have heard Charlotte and Alice, only my voice. "Maybe I was talking to myself then too?"

The ghosts were making me look nuts.

"You know, I thought I saw someone down there with you too. That was impossible, wasn't it?"

"I think he saw us earlier," Alice said.

"That's what it sounds like," Charlotte said.

Yeah, but obviously he couldn't see them now. They were standing right in front of him. Of course, Heather knew what was going on. I really needed to watch talking to the ghosts when other people were around. It was tough, though, because they talked so much that I would become distracted. I'd have a talk with them later about that. Charlotte batted her eyelashes at me as if she knew what I was thinking.

Anyway, it was time to get back to the car. Dylan would wonder what had happened to us.

"Are you all ready to get back to the parking lot? I know you said you needed to find Preston," I said.

"Oh yes, I need to speak with him. Let's go, ladies, shall we?" Ken motioned for us to walk first.

"He's such a gentleman," Charlotte said.

Chapter 26

*Charlotte's Handy-Dandy Tips
for Navigating the Afterlife*

*Remember, animals can see you.
It's good to know you can have the love
of a pet even while haunting a house.*

We headed around the side of the plantation. After all the rain, it had turned out to be a beautiful day. I was just glad that I was alive to see it.

"You ladies must be exhausted. You should get plenty of rest," Ken said as we walked toward the parking lot.

"I think it's been a stressful day for all of us," I said.

"I need a glass of wine and a bubble bath," Heather said. "Oh, and maybe add in some chocolate."

Dylan was speaking with another officer when we reached the lot. He glanced up and waved.

"Thanks for saving us." Heather reached out and hugged Ken.

"You're welcome, but think nothing of it. I just did what I had to do," Ken said.

Heather climbed in the passenger seat of my Buick and rested her head on the back of the seat. She closed her eyes. Charlotte and Alice were already in the backseat. That left me out there to say good-bye to Ken.

"I know Heather said thank you, but I want to say thank you, too. What you did was great."

He looked down. "You're welcome, Cookie. So, what about that coffee?"

Charlotte leaned her head out the window. "Cookie, I swear if you don't say yes . . ."

I smiled. "Sure, call me, okay?"

"You bet."

He turned and headed toward his car. He looked back and waved one last time. When I glanced over toward Dylan, I saw that he was watching me. He hurried across the parking lot.

"How's Heather?" He peeked in the car.

"I think she'll be okay," I said.

He shoved his hands in his pockets. "I have a little more to do here, but would it be okay if I stopped by the shop?"

"I probably won't go back to the shop today," I said.

He looked down.

"But I'll be home if you'd like to stop by later."

He seemed relieved. "Sure, I'd like that a lot. I'll see you soon."

I opened the car door. "Okay, see you soon."

I watched Dylan walk away and then slipped into the car.

"Not a word out of either one of you," I said as I started the engine.

When I glanced in the rearview mirror, I noticed that Charlotte and Alice were smiling. They were both proud of what had happened with Ken and Dylan.

I couldn't say for sure I felt the same. Heather still had her eyes closed, and I didn't want to disturb her.

"There is just one more thing," Alice said.

"What's that?" I asked.

"You need to pay a visit to someone for me. Now that the case is solved, you know."

I'd been so busy thinking about the murder that I'd forgotten.

"Oh yes, I almost forgot, Alice. We will definitely do that. But I think it's best if we wait until after my shower."

"I agree with that," Charlotte said.

The warm water of my shower felt wonderful against my skin, but it did nothing to wash away the thoughts in my mind. It would take a while before my fears and anxiety eased. I was thankful we'd gotten out of there alive. But sad for Nicole.

I forced myself out of the shower, dried off, and went over to my closet. I slipped into a Bleeker Street soft yellow circle skirt dress. It had white trim around the waist and a sleeveless bodice. I finished the outfit with a yellow-and-white chiffon scarf around my neck and yellow sandals. I hoped that the stains would come out of the clothing I'd just taken off.

Wind Song was on her favorite spot on the back of the sofa.

"We'll be back later," I said as I rubbed her head.

She purred in response. Charlotte and Alice were ready to go to Alice's lost love's home. We'd give this one more try, but I wasn't holding out much hope that I'd be able to talk to him this time either. I had to break past the gatekeeper, and that seemed virtually impossible. I slipped behind the wheel. Oddly enough, Charlotte was now in the backseat.

"Why are you back there?" I asked.

"I thought it would be nice if Alice got the front seat for a change," Charlotte said with a wink.

Alice indeed seemed to enjoy her ride up front. I lost myself in thought while navigating the streets to Mr. Bowman's house. Charlotte and Alice talked, but I didn't even notice what they were talking about. After the stress of knowing a killer was on the loose, seeing Jessica arrested was a huge weight off my shoulders. Alice glanced over and smiled. She seemed happy. I hoped for her sake that I could talk with this man.

I pulled up to the curb. Luckily, I didn't see a car in the drive this time. Of course, that didn't mean that his grandson wasn't there.

"How do I look?" Alice asked.

I grimaced. "Well, you look great but he can't see you."

She laughed. "I got you! Of course he can't see me. I'm just pulling your leg."

"Right, well, let's see if we can get past the gate-keeper this time."

I unfastened my seat belt and got out of the car. Alice and Charlotte were already heading up the driveway.

"Hey, wait for me," I called out.

The next-door neighbor was standing in his front yard. He was watching me as he watered the flowers. He looked around to see who I was talk-ing to. When I waved at him, he inclined his head, but turned his attention back to his flowers.

I stepped onto the front porch and up to the front door. Alice tapped her foot against the ground as she motioned for me to ring the bell.

"Okay, I'll do it." I pushed the button and lis-tened to a chime ring throughout the house.

A shuffling noise came from the other side of the door. I held my breath, hoping it wasn't the grandson. I glanced over at Alice, and her face was lit up. She almost had a glow about her, unlike anything I'd seen before.

The lock clicked, and the door inched open. The man standing in front of us definitely wasn't the grandson. He was much older, and I assumed it was Mr. Bowman.

"Is that him?" Charlotte asked Alice.

Alice leaned over for a better view. The inside of the house was dark, so it wasn't easy to see the man's face. I noticed a little bit of gray hair. The rest of his head was bald. He was average height and slender. He wore a light blue button-down shirt and brown pants and brown shoes.

"He isn't young anymore, but he's still just as handsome as ever," Alice said with excitement in her voice.

That was so sweet. I was so glad that he'd answered the door instead of his grandson.

"May I help you?" he asked, looking me up and down.

Now came the hard part, getting him to understand that I wasn't crazy.

Alice motioned. "Go ahead, tell him Alice sent you."

I couldn't lead with that sentence.

"She can't say that," Charlotte said.

He was staring at me, though, so I had to say something soon.

"Hello, sir."

He frowned. I was sure he thought I was trying to sell something.

"My name is Cookie Chanel, and a friend of yours sent me." I glanced over my shoulder.

"And who is your friend, dear?" he asked.

"Well," I cleared my throat. "Her name is Alice Neill."

His eyes widened. It was as if he looked younger just by the mere mention of her name.

"Do you remember her?" I asked.

By the expression on his face, I'd say he remembered her fondly.

"Yes, I remember her." His eyes still had that magic spark.

"Well, she wanted me to give you a message," I said.

He looked sad, then said, "But she passed away."

This was the tricky part. "Yes, I know."

Maybe he wouldn't ask for an explanation. Things would be so much easier that way.

"So you were friends with her?" he asked.

I nodded. It wasn't a lie. I considered Alice a friend. "Yes, she is my friend."

Notice I didn't say *was?* A smiled spread across his face.

"He still has that same great smile," Alice said.

"And all of his teeth too," Charlotte added.

"I regret that I didn't get a chance to speak with her before she passed away," he said.

"There are a lot of things I regret," Alice said.

"Are you friends with her granddaughter?" he asked.

If he started asking questions like that, then this would never work. "I met her briefly." I didn't offer any other details.

"You say she had a message for me?"

"Yes." I didn't know what to say.

The problem was Alice hadn't told me what this message was yet. He looked at me expectantly. Alice needed to give me the message quickly. I couldn't ask her for it in front of him though.

Finally Mr. Bowman said, "Would you like to come inside?"

"Yes, that would be nice."

I stepped into the house. The staircase leading

to the second floor was straight ahead, and it looked as if the living room was on the right. He turned on the small lamp that sat on the table by the door. It looked as if he lived in the house alone. There wasn't much in the way of decorations.

"We can sit in the living room if you'd like." He pointed toward the room.

Alice and Charlotte went in ahead of us.

A plaid sofa was next to the fireplace, and two blue upholstered chairs sat across from it. The room had no TV nor much else other than a few photos on a table by the window. I assumed maybe the people in the photos were his children and grandchildren. I recognized the grandson in one of them. I wondered what had happened to Mr. Bowman's wife.

"Please have a seat." Mr. Bowman gestured toward the sitting area.

I eased down onto one of the blue chairs.

"Would you care for some iced tea?" he asked.

It sounded great. "Yes, that would be lovely."

I hadn't had a chance to eat after what had happened today. Tonight might be a takeout kind of night.

"I'll just go get the drinks," he said and motioned toward the kitchen.

"Thank you."

As he turned to go, he glanced out the window.

"Is that your car?" he pointed.

I smiled. "Yes."

"I had one just like that. Ah, the memories that brings back."

That must have been what Alice had been talking about.

"Well, if you'll excuse me, I'll be right back." He disappeared around the corner.

I leaned over and peeked into the kitchen. Mr. Bowman was getting glasses from the cabinet.

"Alice, you have to tell me what this message is before he comes back."

Charlotte was sitting on the sofa, and Alice was standing by the kitchen door watching Mr. Bowman. She didn't respond.

I whispered again, "Alice."

I couldn't talk any louder.

"Alice!" Charlotte yelled.

Alice looked over at us. I repeated my question. "What is it you want to tell him?"

"Oh yes." She moved over closer to me. "I want to tell him I love him."

Just then Mr. Bowman returned with the tea. I took the cold glass from his outstretched hand. "Thank you."

He sat on the sofa across from me. He had no idea that a ghost was sitting next to him. I took a sip from the glass. "It's very good."

"Thank you. I add enough sugar, then a little more sugar."

I smiled. "That's the best way to make it."

"So what did you want to tell me, dear?"

What was the best way to say this?

"Alice wanted me to tell you that she loves you."

He set his glass on the table beside the sofa. He placed his head in his hands. I couldn't bear to look over at Alice. This was too emotional for me. I didn't deal well with these types of situations.

"Tell him that I should have married him and that I should have never listened to my parents."

After relaying the message, he said, "I shouldn't have let her get away. Don't get me wrong, I loved my wife, God rest her soul, but Alice was the one who got away."

While Alice sat raptly by his side, nodding and smiling, he told me several stories about when she and he had dated. Draining my glass, I realized it was getting dark and time for me to go.

He thanked me for coming over, and I left with a satisfied Alice. Charlotte was sobbing in the back-seat of the car as I drove home. Alice was trying to comfort her. You'd think it would have been the other way around. After all, Alice was the one who'd just said good-bye to her true love. Maybe she'd see him again someday on the other side.

Chapter 27

❧

*Try on a piece of clothing even if you think
it might not be right for you.
Sometimes things look a lot different
when they're on your body.*

The next morning was another bright and sunny day, but that dark cloud of an unsolved mystery was no longer hanging over me or Sugar Creek. Much to Charlotte's chagrin, Dylan had been held up at the crime scene, so he'd been unable to stop by. I dressed in an Yves Saint Laurent turquoise-and-yellow-striped circle skirt. My white cotton blouse had a scalloped neckline and eyelet trim down the front. After my morning routine, I joined Alice and Charlotte in the living room, while Wind Song soaked up a sunbeam on the back of the couch.

"It's time for me to go to work. Are you ladies coming with me today?"

Silence filled the air. Finally Alice said, "It's time for me to leave."

Charlotte was looking down at her feet and wouldn't even look up at me.

"What do you mean?" I asked.

Of course I knew what she meant. Charlotte had stayed, and I just assumed that Alice would too.

"It's time for me to move on. My job here is done."

I sighed. "Yes, I suppose so. I'll miss you."

Charlotte sniffled. Alice looked to Charlotte. "Now don't cry. Just think, you can sit in the front seat again."

Well, I supposed that was something. But when Alice was here, Charlotte had stayed around. Before that she had been popping in and out. I hadn't realized how close the two had become.

"You don't have to go. Why don't you just stay around?" Charlotte asked around her sniffles.

"You and I both know that I need to move on. I have friends and family waiting for me on the other side," Alice said.

Charlotte wiped her eyes and nodded. "I guess you're right."

Charlotte wasn't as tough as I thought.

Alice got to her feet. She still looked as beautiful as the first day I'd seen her at the plantation. Maybe even more so. I wasn't sure where she was going, but I figured she was about to have a lot of fun if she was going to be with her friends and relatives. She walked toward the front door. Charlotte stood and followed her, but stopped at the edge of the room. Alice turned and offered one last wave and smile. Charlotte sniffled, but then pushed her shoulders back and chest forward. She raised her head up high and waved to Alice as she walked out the door.

She didn't bother to open it; she just walked right through. I rushed over to the living room window and pulled back the curtain. I wanted to know where Alice had gone. Was there a ghostly limo waiting for her in the driveway? Would a shuttle bus pick her up? But she was nowhere in sight.

"Good-bye, Alice," I said under my breath.

She was one of the sweetest women I'd ever known. Without her, Nicole's killer probably never would have been brought to justice. Wind Song meowed, as if saying her good-bye too.

Charlotte was standing beside me. I looked at her. "Are you okay?"

She put on her brave face. "Yes, I'll be fine."

I looked to Wind Song and then back to Charlotte. "So, are you two ready to go to the shop?"

Wind Song jumped down from the sofa and went over to her carrier.

"I take that as a yes," I said.

"Let's go help some people look fabulous," Charlotte said as she marched toward the door.

"Sounds like a plan." I grabbed Wind Song and headed out the door.

We piled in the car, but it seemed empty without Alice.

I navigated through town. Sugar Creek was in

full summer mode now. Shorts and flip-flops. Sidewalk sales and yard sales. Barbecues and picnics for everyone. The rest of the summer would be great. And I hoped good sales for me too. When I pulled up to the shop, I noticed Ken leaning up against the side of the building.

"He must be waiting for you." Charlotte didn't even try to hide the excitement in her voice.

"Yes, it does look that way."

I hadn't expected to see him so soon. Sure, he said he would come by, but I wasn't sure if I thought that would really happen. This would have made Alice so happy. I got out of the car and closed the door. I waved as I made my way over to the sidewalk. He stepped away from the building and joined me when I reached the door.

"Good morning. I hope I'm not too early," he said.

His blond hair shone in the bright sun. "I thought I'd come by and see you." He smelled like soap and fresh mint.

I smiled. "I'm glad you did. It's nice to see you under better circumstances."

He flashed the dimples on his cheeks. "Yes, much better this way. I thought maybe you could go for some coffee."

"Yes. Yes. Tell him yes," Charlotte urged.

"I'm sorry. I can't this morning. It's just that I missed so much work yesterday. I'm really behind and need to catch up."

"Look at his face. Will you please stop disappointing this boy?" Charlotte said.

It wasn't like I was trying to do it on purpose.

He studied his shiny brown shoes. "Sure. I can understand that."

Charlotte threw her hands in the air. "That's it. He probably won't ask you again. After getting rejected this many times he will finally just give up."

He'd only asked twice. If he gave up that easily, then did I really want to go for coffee with him? Just then a trim fortyish brunette approached. She looked in the window and then at her watch. She was a little early, but at least I had a customer.

Ken noticed her. "I guess I should let you get to work."

"Yes, I should get in there."

The woman walked away. I hoped that she would return in a few minutes.

"Now you're chasing off customers too?" Charlotte said.

I wanted to respond to her and tell her that I couldn't go to coffee with him and wait on customers at the same time. She would have to decide which one was more important to her. But we'd have that discussion later, once Ken had gone.

"How about tomorrow?" he asked, pulling me back to the conversation.

I smiled. "Sure, I'd like that."

"Well, it's about time you said yes. You're just lucky that he asked again. But what are you going to tell the handsome detective? You can't disappoint him either. I think he really likes you too. See, it's good to have me around. I'm good for your social life. You had none before me."

"So tomorrow morning? How about we met here at eight?"

"That sounds perfect," Charlotte answered.

"Eight will be fine," I said.

That would give me an hour before I had to open the shop.

"Okay, I'll see you then." Ken smiled again and then turned to walk away.

"It's good that you are going to coffee with him. There's really no commitment that way. It's fast. If you don't like him, then you can drink the coffee fast and get out of there. If you like him, then you can sip the coffee."

I looked over at Charlotte as I shoved the keys into the lock. "Thanks for the dating advice."

"You're welcome," she said.

"I meant that sarcastically."

She waved her hand. "It's still valuable."

I supposed she did have a point.

Why had I thought of Dylan when Ken had asked me to coffee? It wasn't like we were dating. He'd never asked me out. Wind Song climbed out of her carrier. Instead of rushing to her favorite spot in the sun, she stayed beside me at the counter.

"Are you hungry?" I asked.

She looked at me and yawned. I prepared her food anyway and placed it on the counter. She turned her head, but still didn't jump down from the counter.

"Okay, suit yourself, I'll just leave it here for you and you can eat when you want to."

She licked her paws and watched me as I sorted

through the mail from yesterday. The bell over the door jingled, and I looked up to see if the customer had returned. Heather walked toward me with the Ouija board under her arm.

"Why do you have that? We don't need it anymore," I said.

"You never know what the cat might have to say."

Heather placed the board on the counter, and Wind Song moved closer to it. She touched the board with her paw.

Heather smirked. "It looks like she wants to use it."

I massaged my temples. "I am outnumbered again. I guess if she wants to do it."

"We thought you'd see it our way."

"Oh, you two are talking now?" I asked.

Heather laughed. "I guess you could say that."

Charlotte looked over my shoulder. "Another cat reading?"

"She must have a message for us if she's so excited to use the board," Heather said as she placed the planchette down.

"Well, I guess we'll see about that," I said.

I had to admit, she did seem eager to use the board. This had better not be another message about the cat food.

"Okay, Wind Song, do your thing." Heather motioned.

Wind Song meowed as if answering her. The cat placed her paws on the board. She pushed the planchette around and around, but she wasn't stopping on anything.

"Maybe she's confused," Heather said.

"Maybe she's trying to decide what to say," Charlotte said.

"Or maybe she really didn't want to use the thing after all."

I was just about to give up when she stopped on a letter. It was the *L*.

"Okay, what next?" Heather asked.

She moved the thing around, and it looked as if she wasn't going to stop again. But finally she stopped on another letter.

It was an *I*. By the time she had finished picking out all the letters, she had spelled out I LIKE THE GUY.

Heather and I exchanged a look.

"What did that mean? Which guy?" she asked.

Wind Song used the planchette again. *Both,* she spelled.

"Both," Heather and I said in unison.

Then we both laughed. Charlotte even joined in our laughter. Wind Song looked up at me as if to say, what are you laughing about? At least now I knew how Wind Song felt about Dylan and Ken. If they brought her treats, she really would be in love. She would probably leave me if they brought her catnip.

"Do you think she's done?" Heather asked.

Wind Song placed her paw on the board and looked up at Heather.

"I guess that means she isn't finished with the board," I said.

"I guess not," Heather said.

"Do you have another message?" I asked.

Wind Song placed her paw on the planchette and moved it around the board again. She seemed to get right to the point this time. She moved with ease around the board, picking out each letter. So far she'd spelled out *House*. Heather and I looked at each other.

"What does that mean?" Heather asked.

I shook my head. "I have no idea. Something at the house, Wind Song?" I asked.

Wind Song kept moving the planchette. I couldn't wait to see what she was going to spell next. The next word was *Around* and after that she simply spelled *The*.

"House around the," Heather said.

"I don't think she's done yet."

"This is taking forever. Can't she do that faster? I want to know what she has to say," Charlotte said.

Wind Song pushed it around until she'd spelled out another word. The last word was *Corner*.

"House around the corner?" Heather asked. "What does that mean?"

"I don't know. There aren't any houses around the corner." It was a few blocks down before there were any houses. There were a few buildings that had been converted into businesses. I wondered if that was what she meant.

"But what about the house?" I asked Wind Song.

Once more Wind Song spelled out a word for us. BEWARE. I swallowed hard.

"Beware of the house around the corner?" I said almost breathlessly. "That sounds ominous."

"Yes, it does," Heather said.

Wind Song didn't move the planchette again this time. Instead, she stepped around the board and over to the dish of food. She started eating. Clearly, she's said what she wanted to say.

"We may never know what she meant," Heather said.

I shrugged. "Maybe she'll give us another message sometime and let us know."

One thing I'd learned, though, was that I should listen to the cat. I didn't know how she did what she did, but I supposed that was something I would never know.

"That will drive me crazy now—not knowing what that cat means by 'house around the corner.'" Charlotte hated an unsolved mystery as much as I did. She would try to coax the cat into using the board again.

The bell caught our attention, and we looked up to see who had entered. Heather grabbed the board.

Dylan held his hand up. "No need to hide the Ouija board from me, ladies. I know you're using it."

I felt heat rush to my cheeks. And I thought all this time that we had been keeping this from him. I should have known that we had done a terrible job of hiding it.

Heather smiled and set the board back on the counter.

"Have you talked to any ghosts?" he asked.

I looked over my shoulder at Charlotte. She shrugged. Dylan pointed toward the board.

"Oh, you mean through the board?"

He laughed. "What did you think I meant?"

I tried to look nonchalant. "The board, of course."

Heather gathered up the board. "It's time for me to get to work. I'll call you soon, Cookie. See you, Detective," she said on her way to the door.

She probably didn't want to be around if I had to explain about actually talking to ghosts. Not with the use of some board, either, but real ghosts.

Wind Song was still on the counter licking her paws after her morning breakfast. When Dylan reached the counter, he stretched down and rubbed her back. She purred and placed her paw on his hand.

"I think she likes you," I said.

He chuckled. "I like her too. I didn't come just to see Wind Song though," he said.

I busied myself holding a shirt just so that he wouldn't catch me smiling too much. Charlotte had taken a seat on the settee. She looked from Dylan to me.

"Something tells me he didn't come in to buy more clothing either."

I thought Charlotte was right about that, although I could have used the business.

Dylan leaned against the counter, and I couldn't help but look up into his big blue eyes. "The reason

I stopped by was to see if you'd like to have lunch with me today."

"Lunch today would be good," I said.

"It's about time you agreed to a date with him."

I wasn't sure a lunch could be considered a date. Though it was a little more than coffee. But Dylan and I had already had a meal together once. This time he'd asked me, and I hadn't just been forced to sit with him because all the seats were taken like when we'd shared the breakfast. I guess that did make it different.

"Good." He smiled. "I know this great place across town."

"Something different than Glorious Grits?" That was almost like a real date.

"Well, what are you going to do now?" Charlotte asked from her spot on the settee. "You have both of these handsome men asking you out and vying for your attention."

Now was not the time I wanted to think about that. I'd have to think about it later.

"Don't get me wrong, it's certainly not a bad situation to be in," Charlotte said as she studied her fingernails.

Dylan was watching me. He followed my gaze. "I thought I saw a customer coming in." I hadn't been looking at the window, and he probably knew that.

Just then the bell on the door caught our attention. We spotted Shiloh walking toward us. I wasn't exactly happy to see her. It brought up too many memories that were fresh in my mind. I had wanted to push the memories to the back of my mind for a while.

She had a big box in her arms and a smile on her face. "Good morning, Cookie. Hello, Detective." Her voice was sugar sweet.

"Good morning." My greeting was filled with suspicion.

I still wasn't sure that I trusted her.

"I brought back the clothing."

Dylan took the box from her arms and placed it on the counter.

"That isn't all of them, of course. The rest are in my car. I can't thank you enough for all that you did for the movie. You made the cast and me look good."

That wasn't what she'd said before. When she thought I wasn't listening, she'd been critical of my clothing selections. I wouldn't hold that against her now, I supposed. If she truly wanted to be nice now, I would put the past behind us.

"You're welcome," I said.

"She should be nice to you now after how nasty she's been," Charlotte said.

"I can help you get the rest of the boxes," Dylan offered.

"Thanks. That's so sweet of you."

I walked outside with Dylan and Shiloh, and we carried the cartons inside.

"Everything is there," she said. "If you want to look it over and make sure."

I didn't want her to wait around while I checked out all the items. I would just take her word for it.

"That won't be necessary," I said.

Shiloh checked the time on her cell. "Well, I guess I'd better go. I have a plane to catch."

"See you around," I said.

Shiloh walked out of the shop. I had been excited for the movie crew to be in Sugar Creek. Now I was thankful that they were gone.

"So all the film stars and crew left?" I asked.

Dylan shoved his hands in his pockets. "Yes, they cleared out this morning. I guess Shiloh was the last to leave. What you did for Nicole was great, but I hope you never do that again."

"I think the murder investigations in Sugar Creek are over, so we shouldn't have anything to worry about." I cut a quick look at Charlotte.

She winked.

"You're probably right, but just the same."

"I'll try to stay out of it from now on." I crossed my fingers behind my back.

He tapped the counter. "Okay, so I'll see you back here at twelve?"

"Yes, that will be fine." I wondered if my cheeks had turned red.

He smiled again before heading for the door.

"I'm looking forward to lunch," Charlotte said.

I whipped around to glare at her.

She held her hands up. "Just kidding. I'll stay away this time." Charlotte laughed.

"Thank you," I said as I picked up the morning newspaper.

The front-page story was about the murder.

There was a picture with me in the background at the parking lot next to my car. The reporters had asked me to talk with them, but I'd declined. It wasn't something I really wanted to discuss. Of course, the main photo was of Jessica. That picture of her face with the wild hair and mascara-covered cheeks would haunt me in my sleep. To the side was a photo of her from the movie, when she'd looked glamorous. What a stark contrast.

I placed the paper down and looked over at Charlotte. "So it's just you and me now."

She tapped her fingers on the seat. "That's true. It's kind of quiet. You know, without a murder to solve or anything."

"Well, I do have a lot of work around here to do."

She jumped up from the seat. "Yes, and I need to help you get more customers. There are more ads to place and blogs to post. We need to advertise a sale or special event."

Yes, it looked as if Charlotte wasn't going anywhere anytime soon.

I busied myself with folding shirts and placing dresses on hangers. I needed to redo the window too. Wind Song had taken her place in the sun now. She was content. Everything was back to normal. Just the way that I liked it. I had pulled out a stack of invoices and settled on the stool behind the counter.

But the bell over the door pulled me away from the work almost instantly. A customer entered. It was the brunette who had been by earlier when

Ken was here. I was glad that she had returned. She had stylish brown hair that fell just to her shoulders. She wore jeans that looked expensive, with a white tank top and white sandals. Charlotte hurried toward the counter—I knew she didn't want to miss this conversation.

The woman scanned the entire shop within a couple seconds, then focused her attention on me again. "Good morning. I hope I'm not too early. I came by earlier and you weren't open yet."

"Welcome to It's Vintage, Y'all. You're not too early. May I help you find something?"

"Oh, I just wanted to come in and look around. The window display was just so fabulous that I couldn't resist."

"Thank you." My voice was packed with pride after her compliment.

Charlotte was looking the woman up and down.

"I'm new in town," she said. "I just moved here last week."

"Ask her where she's from," Charlotte said as she stared at the woman.

"I bought the beauty shop here in Sugar Creek."

"Really? Where did you move from?" I asked to make Charlotte happy.

"I came from Tallahassee, Florida. That's where I grew up. But I figured it was time for a change."

Charlotte held up her hand. "Oh no. You don't just pick up and move to Sugar Creek for no reason. You need to get to the bottom of this."

I couldn't ask that many questions all at once.

Charlotte would have to wait. I had to ease into the questions.

"Well, I'm going to look around," she said.

"Sure." I smiled. "Let me know if you need anything."

When she walked away, Charlotte said, "Why didn't you find out more about her?"

"I will, but you have to give me time," I whispered.

The woman brought a turquoise and lime-green cotton Lilly Pulitzer dress up to the counter. "I just have to have this dress."

"Nice selection." I took the dress from her.

"Ask her now," Charlotte said.

"Oh, I forgot to ask your name," I said as I rang up her dress.

"My name is Brooke House."

"House around the corner," Charlotte said at the same time as I was thinking it.

Like I said, I should always listen to the cat.

An Excerpt from Cookie Chanel's Fashion Blog

Popular Fashion Pieces from Each Decade

When shopping for vintage clothing, it helps to know the year of the fashion you're looking for, that way you'll be better equipped to judge its value.

1920s: The roaring twenties was the era of the flapper and brought big changes in fashion.

Popular items included flapper dresses, cloche hats, finger wave short hairstyles, pants, ankle strap button shoes, and stockings.

1930s: The thirties were a time of economic struggle, but despite that, clothing was still fashionable.

Popular items included floral feed sack dresses, suede gloves with matching bag and shoes, slinky silks, bolero jackets and fitted sweaters, and padded shoulders.

1940s: This was another time for big change in

the fashion world. With the war came the need for rationing, and that spawned creativity.

Popular styles in the forties included jumper dresses worn over blouses and sweaters, wedge heels, wide-leg trousers, and hair snoods.

1950s: The fifties brought a feminine and tailored look. Dresses were the most common women's clothing worn.

Popular items in the fifties included strapless cocktail dresses, pedal pushers, crinoline or swing skirts, pencil skirts, Bermuda shorts, Peter Pan collars, and saddle shoes.

1960s: Many changes took place with fashion in the sixties. Different styles came into being, such as hippie and mod. The success of the space program also influenced fashion with the use of metallic fabrics and plastic.

Popular items from the sixties included knee-high white patent leather go-go boots, miniskirts or dresses, low hipster pants, bell-bottom jeans, and tie-dye.

1970s: Fashion in the seventies had transitions from sixties pieces and was influenced by movies and celebrities.

Some popular items in the seventies included hot pants, platform shoes, leisure suits, and denim decorated with embroidery, colorful stitching, or other embellishments. Also popular: macramé bags, gauzy cotton dresses, gypsy tops and caftans, tube tops, crop tops—and don't forget the bell-bottoms.

1980s: Fashion in the eighties was influenced by color. Lots of fashion in the eighties was unisex.

Popular styles in the eighties included jackets with shoulder pads, acid-wash jeans, bomber jackets, leg warmers, Members-Only jackets, neon colors, off-the-shoulder tops, jellies, stirrup pants, parachute pants, scrunch socks, fingerless gloves, and Jordache jeans.

1990s: The casual look was popular in the nineties. Nineties fashion also included recycled styles from the previous decades.

Popular styles in the nineties included tapered pants, cargo pants, biker shorts, Air Jordans, ripped jeans, Hypercolor T-shirts, and knee-high socks.

Tips for Living with a Psychic Cat

1. Embrace the cat's talent. You might find it can be fun or the cat can help you find your missing car keys.
2. Help the cat by providing tarot cards or Ouija board. Sure, I was skeptical at first, but so far my kitty's messages have been accurate. I could do without the constant reminders to buy gourmet cat food though.
3. Remember that allowing the cat to embrace his or her psychic ability might also provide stress relief for the kitty. It could even be better than catnip. Listen to the cat.
4. As I mentioned earlier, your cat will probably use this talent to communicate messages. You'll know when she wants the litter changed or when that fur ball is a problem. The kitty will be outspoken, but at least you'll never have to guess what she wants again.
5. Speaking of being outspoken, don't ignore the cat's requests. Trying to sneak in the cat food she doesn't like will not end well

for you. Trust me—I learned this the hard way.

6. When your psychic cat warns you about strangers, you should listen. That message could save your life.

All of these tips can be applied to nonpsychic cats too. Now that you have these helpful tips, I hope life with your new psychic friend is a breeze.

Don't miss the next delightful
Haunted Vintage Mystery by Rose Pressey

HAUNT COUTURE AND GHOSTS GALORE

Coming from Kensington Publishing Corp.
in Fall 2015!

Keep reading to enjoy a preview excerpt . . .

Chapter 1

The ghost of Charlotte Meadows typically stalked me everywhere I went. Today she had been suspiciously absent. Trouble followed her, though, and I figured at any minute I'd become aware of her presence. Now wasn't exactly the best timing. I was a little occupied with my current project.

Dresses were scattered about the floor. Shoes were piled into a corner like a mountain ready to topple at any moment. I'd never been behind the scenes at a fashion show before, and the frantic pace was a little frightening. Models slipped into the outfits with ease though, so the frenzied pace didn't seem to affect them. I tried to stay out of the way, but the space backstage was cramped, making it extremely difficult. Picking out a vintage Pierre Balmain red scarf, I tossed it to one of the models. She caught the scarf mid-air and in a fluid movement draped it around her neck. Now the outfit was complete.

When I was a teenager, I'd thought about modeling, but I never had the grace. Plus, at five-foot-two, I wasn't tall enough for the runway. That hadn't stopped me from loving fashion. I put effort into every outfit I wore. Like today, my sleeveless blouse was navy blue with white polka dots and my fifties skirt was lipstick red with accordion-style pleats. I'd taken the time to style my dark hair into victory rolls too.

Dressing the part was key to running a successful vintage-clothing shop. That and the fact that I loved all things vintage. I even drove a 1948 red Buick convertible that my grandfather had left to me. It was the bee's knees. My name is Cookie Chanel, and I am a vintage-clothing connoisseur. I own the It's Vintage, Y'all boutique in Sugar Creek, Georgia.

My mother said I got my style and love of fashion from my grandmother. Granny Pearl had been the one who started calling me Cookie because the moniker fit so well with Chanel—that and she loved Coco Chanel. My given name is Cassandra, but everyone calls me Cookie.

Never had I thought that running a vintage-clothing shop would bring so much adventure into my life. Maybe I should have taken some time off after helping a movie company with their vintage costumes. After all, there had been a murder on set, but I liked to keep busy, so I'd moved right on to another project.

I'd received a call from Cindy Johnson asking if I'd like to help her raise money for her anti-domestic abuse charity, Speak Out. Of course I agreed. The ghost that had latched onto me thought it was a good idea too. She'd practically insisted. I'd met Charlotte Meadows at her estate sale. She'd been murdered and demanded that I find her killer. Now she wouldn't leave. Charlotte hadn't been the only ghost I'd encountered either, but I hoped now that interacting with the spirit world was all behind me. Maybe Charlotte would eventually move into the next dimension. Around the same time that I met Charlotte, a gorgeous white cat found me. It sounded crazy, but the cat communicated with us by using tarot cards and a Ouija board. So maybe I wasn't getting away from the supernatural anytime soon.

Cindy had put me in touch with Melanie Lee. Melanie worked at the fashion design school in Atlanta. She had designed clothing that we would feature in today's fashion show. I had been asked to pair vintage items with her new garments. That sounded like fun to me, so I had agreed. Melanie had been running around backstage furiously trying to get everything in place on time.

"Where is the red dress?" she yelled at no one in particular.

Melanie's brown hair had started the day in an updo, but now the left side had fallen to her shoulder. The aqua-colored wrap dress she wore was one of her own designs.

I eased over to her as if she were a ferocious lion. "Melanie, do you need my help or should I go have a seat in the auditorium?"

She whipped around with fire in her eyes. "What do you want . . . oh, Cookie. No, I think we have it from here. Thank you."

Melanie turned around and stormed off. I had put all the vintage items with their coordinating outfits, so I guessed there was nothing left for me to do. I felt as if I was just in the way in the confined space. One less body back there would be a good thing.

On the other side of the room, I spotted someone I knew. Actually, I'd only met her a couple times now. Brooke House had recently moved to town and opened a beauty salon around the corner from my shop. She was doing hair and makeup for the show today. Brooke had styled her own chestnut-colored hair in soft waves that fell to her shoulders. Strands of loose wisps pushed forward toward her heart-shaped face. She wore dark blue Hudson jeans on her slender frame and a wine-colored sleeveless Susana Monaco blouse.

Brooke must have felt my eyes on her. She glanced in my direction and frowned. After a couple seconds, she attempted a halfhearted smile. I tossed my hand up in a wave. My cat had warned me to watch out for her. Wind Song had told me to avoid her. But that was hard to do in a town the size of Sugar Creek. Anyway, more about my psychic cat later.

As I headed toward the door, a gorgeous brunette with delicate features stopped me. She wore a form-fitting black with red polka dot Christian Dior dress that I had provided for the show. I'd paired a vintage black motorcycle jacket with the dress to give the outfit an edge. Her ensemble was entirely vintage except for the fact that she wasn't wearing shoes. Her hair was styled in a bob with loose curls falling gently next to her face.

"I can't find the shoes." Her voice was in panic mode.

What was I supposed to do?

"Um, I don't know where your shoes are."

"Well, what am I supposed to do, go out there barefoot?" She placed her hands on her hips.

Somehow I remembered this model's name. I'd met a lot of models over the course of the past couple days, but Hannah O'Neil stood out from the rest. Maybe it was because she yelled a lot and had been known to throw things at people. Like my grandfather would have said, she was as mean as a rattlesnake. I had a feeling if she had her shoes right now, she would throw them at me.

A petite blonde stomped over to us with a pair of black stilettos in her hand. "Here are the shoes. And remember to put them back in the bag and hang them with your outfit when the show is over."

The four-and-a-half-inch Jimmy Choo heels made me want to drool. Hannah snatched them from Meaghan's hands, obviously not impressed by the gorgeous shoes. She was probably used to wearing stylish items like that.

"It's about damn time," Hannah said as she stormed off.

"She has such a pleasant personality, don't you think?" Meaghan rolled her eyes.

"She's a real doll," I said.

Meaghan McKinney was Melanie Lee's assistant. I didn't envy her job. She worked under this kind of pressure all the time. Melanie was trying to make it big with her designs, and that meant a lot of stress. I didn't see why she wouldn't be successful either, because the items I'd seen so far were gorgeous. It didn't look as if Meaghan had had much time to decide on her outfit for the day. Her jeans were wrinkled, and her plain white T-shirt was half tucked in. One of her sneakers' laces was untied.

"Sorry about that." She blew the bangs out of her eyes.

"It's okay. I guess you're used to it by now."

"I wouldn't say used to it, but I've learned how to deal with it. I should have become a veterinarian like I'd first intended." She shook her head.

"Meaghan!" Melanie yelled from behind a rack of clothing.

"I'd better go." She rushed off when Melanie yelled her name again.

I stepped out from backstage and took a seat at the front of the stage. The place was packed, and I was excited about the turnout. Being a part of the action had been thrilling, and it would be fun to see the final outcome. I just hoped none of the models tripped while onstage. A woman in her midthirties sat next to me. She had short black hair and wore a form-fitting red-and-white dress that hit just below the knees. I didn't recognize the designer of the dress, but I recognized the woman from being backstage earlier in the day.

I'd seen her leaving a red dress on one of the racks. Shandra Jordan also designed clothing, but I wasn't sure if she had any pieces in today's show. She noticed me watching her.

"Hello." Her tone let me know she wondered why I was staring at her.

"I'm excited for the show. Do you have clothing featured in the show?" I asked.

"No," she said drily.

The music pumped a little too loudly from speakers behind the stage, and the models streamed out one by one. I was happy to see that they had all worn my vintage pieces correctly. None of the items had gotten mixed up with the wrong outfits. The show passed quickly, and everyone clapped as Melanie emerged onstage and took a bow. Shandra snorted. I looked over at her. A scowl covered her face as she stared at Melanie. At least I thought she was staring at her. I wondered what that was all about. She didn't look happy with Melanie.

Now that the show had finished, I had to go backstage and make sure all of the clothing items I'd brought were returned. The items were delicate because of their age, and I wanted to make sure they weren't tossed around too much. I liked to think of the items as my babies.

When I walked backstage, the models were feverishly removing the clothing and tossing the items onto the floor, changing into their own outfits. So far I hadn't spotted Melanie or her assistant, Meaghan. I wanted to congratulate them on a job well done.

"Has anyone seen Melanie?" I asked.

Most of the models ignored me; then again, it was noisy back there, and maybe they hadn't heard me. A couple of women nearby glanced at me and shook their heads.

I moved through the small space, weaving around the models.

"Please return the vintage items to the rack by the door," I yelled so they would hear me.

Again, they didn't pay me any attention. I cringed at the way some of them were handling the clothing. I would thank Melanie and then hurry back in here to get my items before there was a disaster.

As I stepped out from the back room, a small equipment room was on one side of the hallway and on the other side was a sound room. I checked both spaces, but couldn't find Melanie. At the end of the hall was an exit door. Maybe she'd stepped outside.

When I opened the door to the outside, I looked to my left and spotted Hannah. She was staring at the ground. I followed her gaze and spotted Melanie facedown on the ground. Blood had pooled under her body. My stomach clenched, and the smell of rotting trash from the nearby cans didn't help. At that moment Hannah looked up at me. Her face was pale and haunted.

"I think she's dead," Hannah said.

"Well, pick my peas, you've discovered another dead person," came a familiar voice.

I knew it wouldn't take long before Charlotte caught up with me.